CLOU

M000080160

- By -

Nicholas Ifkovits

Also by Nicholas Ifkovits

Cloud Drops
Other Dreams
Harmony's Angel
Strange Change

To Jessica, Thanks!
Vaya Con Dios.
Nick
02-24-06

Thank you
For serving!

Counter-Force ™

Press

Counter-Force Press
POB 138
Mesa, CO 81643-0138

Library of Congress Control Number: 2001-129338

Title: CLOUD DROPS / Second Edition / Revised

ISBN: 0-9651700-5-5

Manufactured in the United States of America.
   10   9   8   7   6   5   4   3   2   1

Cover art by Debra "Dandelion Deb" Alire.

— Dedicated to the poor in spirit —

> Most of the pain in the world that human beings endure comes not from God, nor from Satan. It comes from other human beings.
> — Nicholas Ifkovits

Hello

CLOUD DROPS

1

NIGHT-FLIGHT

> ... and the wheels were lifted up over
> against them: for the spirit of the living
> creatures was in the wheels.
> - EZEKIEL 1:20

Slowing to 50,000 miles per hour, the UFO enters the upper stratosphere with the circle of its 18 fiery bluish-white lights appearing to blink. But it is only an illusion created as the huge disc, passing through the mists and vapors at supersonic speeds, arcs towards the Earth and begins its descent.

From the Earth far below it might appear as an enormous shooting star. Passing through the NORAD electronic defense shield, it will not appear on any radar screens. The beams of radar simply pass right through rather than being reflected back.

Each of the 18 lights is actually a separate entity, a creature of electromagnetic energy which, when traveling, takes the form of a fiery wheel. And each of these revolving wheels is linked to the other 17 in a perfect circle measuring 54 feet across.

There is no thunder of jet engines or mechanical parts, just a quiet humming as they move across the sky, the fires of their souls waxing and waning from a brilliant whitish-blue to deep orangish-red with energies exerted or withheld. The humming is their soft, communal singing as they methodically go about their business.

An air force jet plying the night skies whose pilot might catch a brief glimpse will see a brightly illuminated disc of some kind of shiny, grayish metal. Again it is only illusion, created by the refracted light of the 18 revolving wheels and the pilot's own mind and eyes which are trained to see lights moving through the sky as attached to some mechanized flying machine. Actually, there is no metal, only Living Beings. And the linking of the wheels is in fact a "joining of hands" of each of them.

In a flash the glowing "disc" is gone, for it eludes all Earthling aircraft in an endless game of hide-and-seek. And unaffected by G-forces as the Beings of the "spacecraft" are, it eludes even America's high performance F-15 jet fighters quite easily, there one moment and gone the next, capable of making radical directional changes even at tens of thousands of miles per hour. For example it can be zipping along at 75,000 miles per hour and simply stop in a cloud. Or, traveling along horizontally, in the blink of an eye it can change to a vertical course in an impossible square-turn maneuver, gaining miles of altitude in fractions of a second.

Of course sometimes they merely dematerialize, although this is the least favored choice of the Beings because it involves a dis-linking and scattering, which induces a mild apprehension. They like to remain together as one. And so dematerializing is only employed in emergency situations when their presence might cause a startled airline pilot, for instance, to engage a radical collision-avoidance maneuver which could result in injury to passengers, or even a tragic accident.

In this situation the unsuspecting pilot never even has a chance to flinch before the "spacecraft" is gone, his own aircraft experiencing a slight bumping as it passes through the lingering magnetic field of the expanded, "de-atomized" bodies of the Beings. Seconds later the pilot can only shake his head and wonder, had he really *seen* anything at all? By then the 18 creatures are pulling themselves together, regrouping hundreds of miles away.

These 18 are only one of many squadrons, an elite force that returns to Earth most often on rescue missions. And although the imprint and image of each of their personalities is as distinctive and recognizable as a thumbprint, in their present form of electromagnetic energy and light there is no discernible difference between the men and women. These are sexless creatures, unequipped with sexual organs. They do not procreate. They do not marry. Although child-like in their behavior, given as they are to pranks and children's games, they carry within them the wisdom of the ages. These are eternal creatures. Timeless. Ageless. Forever young.

Incapable of perversion, they tend to be quite open and uninhibited about their affections, expressing it verbally with a boldness one sees only in young children. Holding hands is also quite common. Thus, these go about carefree and happy, and as often as not break into song with the latest rhyme someone among them has made up, as if they didn't have a care in the world. And generally they don't, for they answer to no one except their King, and he's usually quite warm and easygoing with these, his "adopted" children.

Over northern Minnesota the disc, its 18 bluish-white lights revolving, goes into a wide, sweeping banked turn, still descending as it changes to a southwesterly course and heads straight for Houston, Texas. Far below, the pinwheels

of twinkling lights that mark out the urban centers of the
Midwest come into view, reminding the travelers of distant
galaxies in deep space and giving them a mild jolt of home-
sickness. But no one dwells on it or even mentions it.
They've got a job to do.

CLOUD DROPS

2

UNSEEN FRIENDS

> And the men which journeyed with him
> stood speechless, hearing a voice, but
> seeing no man.
>   - ACTS 9:7

It was happening again. That strange urging, as if something were beckoning, calling him out to the backyard. Curious, a little frightened, six-year-old Ledyard Patterson dropped the Nintendo *GameBoy* he was playing with and went to the playroom window. It was dusk. A huge Texas sun the color of warm blood was poised on the horizon beyond the rolling green carpet of golf course that bordered his family's private, two-acre compound, built in the midst of the 6,000-acre Christian Condensed Ministry's campus, founded by his televangelist father, Pat Patterson.

He had never been on the golf course before. In fact he was hardly allowed out in the yard alone. His parents were paranoid that some deranged person disgruntled with his famous father's rather dogmatic fundamentalist theology might slither from the urban slime of nearby Houston and attack or kidnap the boy. Still, what was it? Ledyard peered around the room. It was so strange, this weird feeling suddenly upon him.

The room was cool. He could feel the coolness, but he was warm. Tingling warm. And that strange urging. Something was outside and it was calling to him and suddenly he wanted to be there. *Had* to be there. He wanted to know. What?

The little boy crept to the door, eased it open, stuck his head out and looked up and down the hall. His parents were out for the evening. He was glad of that. Otherwise, the thought crossed his mind, he'd never make it outside. Like the last time....

Elly, the maid, was down in the living room reading. It would be easy to sneak out the backdoor. Wearing his one-piece baby-blue pajamas with the feet in them and a zipper up the front, Ledyard tiptoed down the hall, down the stairs, and with his back against the wall, slipped into the kitchen and stopped at the backdoor. Determined that before being discovered he would at least make it to the decorative split-rail fence that separated their yard from the golf course, the little blond, blue-eyed six-year-old reached up, twisted the doorknob and slipped out, gently closing the door behind him.

It was cool and shadowy, the rush of the wind rising and falling as it rustled the leaves of the towering oaks that graced their meticulously landscaped estate. The huge red sun was half-sunken into the Earth now. Underfoot the grass was soft, cool and damp, immediately soaking through the feet of his pajamas.

Driven by one simple urge, to find out what was out there in the gathering gloom that seemed to be calling to him, Ledyard glanced back at the kitchen door once, then scampered across the huge expanse of rolling lawn to the rear of the yard.

He ran to the left, down a slight slope, and stopped at the split-rail fence. He stood for a long moment, staring, feeling, his arms held away from his sides as if he were trying to touch the very air around him. The fiery red orb of the sun was slipping. Soon it would be gone and he'd be left alone in the dark.

The boy slowly lowered his arms, every sense alive, electric, his hearing, smell, and taste sharp, his eyes searching. It wasn't *here,* but it was close, whatever it was, for he could clearly feel it.

Almost catlike, he lifted each foot very high and took one broad, carefully placed step after the other, as if he were some prehistoric hunter stalking prey. Making his way along the fence and up the slope without a sound, the little boy suddenly froze in mid-stride and looked up, his right foot held high. Slowly, unconsciously, the foot came down and he stood firmly, feet apart, the slightest hint of a smile playing on his face as he gazed up at the walnut tree he had stopped beneath.

And then that "glow" was upon him again, like up in the playroom when the air had felt so cool and he so warm, with his entire being engulfed in a tingling sensation. Gradually his breathing became shallow and steady as if he were falling asleep. Total calm. Total contentment. Yet his mind was alert. At last he spoke softly. "Hello? Is anyone there?"

Now, if someone had been hiding nearby listening and watching they would have seen and heard a silly little boy talking to a tree. When the tears began rolling down his cheeks they would have thought him disturbed or severely depressed, not knowing, of course, that his were tears of joy. And it would be through no fault of their own, as well, when they failed to hear the tree *talking back* to the child, for everyone knows that trees don't talk.

CLOUD DROPS

3

OTHER WORLD

> *And he said unto them, whosoever shall receive this child in my name receiveth me....*
>
> *- LUKE 9:48*

Even among the Elite no one was anxious to walk the Earth again, for to do so involved donning an "Earth Unit" of flesh and blood. To tread the heavens above the clouds and occasionally pressurize the air to distract a criminal, or chase off a gang of "Other Ones" trying to stir up trouble for some unfortunate soul, well that was one thing. But once returned to an Earth Unit—to the flesh—there was only one way out again and that was to die, being, as it were, the only way to shed the vessel of flesh and blood and return to the sky.

Even for someone secure in the knowledge of the outcome, even for someone who has once before experienced "death," it was still a traumatic and frightening thing to contemplate. Such is the great force which is the will to survive, an integral part of the flesh that knowledge alone cannot overcome, not to mention leaving loved ones and the bliss of heaven to return to the cold, hungry, sometimes brutal struggle for survival on Earth. In fact returning to the flesh was rarely done and required of no one.

And so when Cambian landed upon the front lawn of the King's personal dwelling in response to a request for a volunteer, a code-six voucher attached indicating a return to terra firma via the flesh, the King was well pleased.

Cambian straightened his gray cotton shorts, which had twisted around a bit upon landing, started across the grass, scampered up three stone steps, crossed a huge expanse of front porch with four marble columns, and stopped before the tall oak doors. Hesitantly lifting the brass knocker, he let it fall once with a heavy bang.

Expecting to be greeted by the housekeeper of the day, when the double doors swung aside and the King himself stood there smiling, Cambian froze, mouth agape. When the realization of who stood before him sunk in, Cambian muttered, "Forgive me, Lord," and quickly dropped to his knees and bowed his head to the floor.

For a moment all was quiet, then the King's head fell back with a hearty laugh. At the laughter Cambian chanced a peek, tilting his head slightly to catch a glimpse with his left eye.

Still chuckling, the golden-tousled curls of his head shining light like a gold crown even in the cool shadow of the porch, Jesus said mildly, "My, my, Cambian, aren't we being formal today!" Then he stooped, gathered the youth into his muscular arms and tossed him high into the air, caught him and smiled broadly at Cambian's happy laughter. Kissing the boy once, he swung him up on his shoulders and carried him into the house, kicking one side of the double doors closed with the heel of his foot. Naturally the other door followed suit, swinging shut with a sound *click*.

Striding through the elegantly appointed mansion with Cambian atop his shoulders, Jesus said, "I'm glad you responded, Cambian, because my need for a volunteer is linked to a project you're already involved in. Shall we have lunch and discuss it?"

Cambian, a nickname he had acquired as a popular descendant of the Cambodian people, gulped, stammering, "W-Why yes, of course, sir." He hadn't expected a lunch invitation. To dine with the Lord was considered a great honor.

"To the bath, then!" the Lord exclaimed, for it was customary to wash before meals. It might be added, to these creatures eating was only a pleasant pastime. They had no *need* of food, their bodies merely burning off whatever was consumed without the necessity of it going through any gastric process. To break bread with someone was also a formal means of demonstrating friendship. Furthermore, washing was not merely a hands-cleansing chore but a communal recreational amusement that everyone enjoyed, as the washing facilities would attest to.

Out back was a tropical garden, the centerpiece a natural, two-acre pool. There, Jesus set Cambian down. Crystal clear warm-water springs gushed up from craggy rock formations near the rear, feeding the pool in three splashing waterfalls. At the far end the water spilled over the top, carried away in a sandy creek sparkling in the sun as it twisted and turned through a distant valley lush with emerald-green forest.

With the laughter of a child Cambian whipped off his shorts and kicked them high into the air with one foot, watched as they plopped onto a nearby marble bench, then ran up the winding path to the pool and dived in, shouting, "Come on, Lord!"

Grinning, Jesus slipped out of his gleaming white, gold-embroidered robe, neatly draped it over the bench beside

Cambian's shorts, sprinted up the path and dived into the pool.

After a short intense game of water polo they called it quits at a score of seven to seven. Climbing out of the pool, they showered briefly beneath the warm waters of the falls and returned to the bench where they had left their garments.

While waiting to dry, the water droplets clinging to their tanned bodies sparkling in the sun, they got into a fast and furious game of slap-hands in which Jesus' reflexes proved to be somewhat quicker. True, they could have simply vaporized the water droplets in a fraction of a second and dressed immediately, but they were enjoying the warm sunshine. And since they had all the time in eternity there was no rush.

They lunched on broiled whitefish and lightly buttered steamed rice with fresh sliced mushrooms and pearl onions, taking the meal in the cool shade of the expansive veranda that overlooked the garden with its pool and splashing waterfalls.

After the food was set before them, their crystal goblets filled with iced papaya juice, and the servant had withdrawn, Jesus spoke quietly, cutting into the tender fish with the side of his fork. "So, I understand you managed to establish contact with young Ledyard Patterson."

"Yes sir," Cambian answered, lifting a forkful of the flaky, delectable fish.

Jesus swallowed, his fork hovering over the rice dish. "And how did that go?"

"Good, sir. He was very receptive."

"Good," Jesus answered, "but you do realize it's his father we want to win to our cause, don't you?"

Cambian cleared his throat. "Uh, that is a little confusing to me, sir. I mean, his father's always talking about you on television."

"*Using* me would be a better way of putting it. And getting rich for his efforts, too. But the most disturbing thing, Cambian, is that he's generating a massive following and polarizing the people, one religion against the other. The irony, of course, is that just when nations are finally learning to settle their political differences peacefully, this cheap television pop-star and others like him are going to end up splitting nations along religious lines!"

"Which side are we on, sir?"

"We're not on any side, Cambian," Jesus answered, dipping into the rice dish. Gesturing with his fork he added, "Eat."

Cambian took a bite. "And this guy Patterson...."

"Has them worshipping the religion instead of the God," Jesus interjected. "And he's certainly *not* proclaiming *my* teachings, nor those of God. Neither is the Pope or any of the rest of them for that matter. Religion is all about politics, power and money. Always has been and apparently always will be. That's why I blew-up that time and overturned the money-changers' tables."

"Uh-huh," Cambian nodded. "I see what you're getting at. If we get to the boy early enough before he's brainwashed...."

"Right. He's heir to a powerful religious empire. And one that shows no signs of letting up, I might add. If we can just keep tabs on him and little by little bring him in, well, maybe his father will come around and maybe he won't, but at least one of *our* guys will be well-positioned when Patterson retires."

Cambian bowed his head, "In your service, my Lord, I pray always keep me."

Jesus waved the pleasantries aside, his face growing somber. "This is a long-term project. You'll be working with the boy over the next ten years or so. And then, if it looks like the right thing to do we'll probably go for something dramatic like a touch down—in the flesh—thus my request for a volunteer with the code-six voucher attached."

Again Cambian bowed his head. "In your service, my Lord."

Jesus smiled. "Thank you, Cambian. Then the assignment is yours. That is, if we decide to go through with it. In the meantime just keep coaxing the boy along like you've been doing." As an afterthought he added, "Oh, and plan on maybe setting up an out-of-body experience for him when he's about ten just to lock him in and get him ready for the big one." He paused. "Have you ever done one of those before? An out-of-body?"

"No sir," Cambian shook his head. "But I've got lots of time to get the team together and practice."

"Good," Jesus said conclusively. "Don't let your food get cold."

At the great front door of the Lord's house Jesus took Cambian in a final embrace, then held him at arm's length by the shoulders. "Now, tomorrow come by the House of Kings and we'll make a formal announcement concerning our decision." Then he said goodbye and sent the youth off with an affectionate clap on the shoulder.

CLOUD DROPS

4

HOLY MOSES

> *...as they went on and talked, a chariot of fire appeared, ...and Elijah went up by a whirlwind into heaven.*
>
> *- II Kings 2:11*

Cambian could have flown to his residence and arrived within seconds, but it was such a beautiful summer day and he was feeling so contented with his decision that he decided to walk the 40 miles home.

There were no roads, only footpaths, as there were no wheeled vehicles on the planet except as toys for the amusement of youngsters, where wheeled vehicles were restricted to a 400,000-acre mechanical amusement park called Greasy City (which was actually very clean).

Waving to a group of boys and girls playing soccer beneath a perfect blue sky dotted with cotton-puff clouds, Cambian set off across the park. The youngsters paused briefly, returning the wave, then resumed their game as Cambian entered the lush, primeval forest and followed a winding footpath through dappled sunlight.

Two hours later, deep in the forest, he decided to stop in a grassy clearing and soak his feet in the cool waters of a stream that thundered over shiny black boulders. He had spent many a summer day with a companion or two beside just such a stream, lounging on his back in the soft green grass with a leg up on one knee, a fishing pole dangling between his big and middle toes, waiting in perfect peace for a nice fat brook trout to snag the line.

Contemplating the prospect of having to return to Earth via the flesh, he was having second thoughts. Once in there would be no way out except through the long, arduous process of life itself. (To self-destruct was absolutely forbidden.) On the other hand things could go very easily. After all it was Earthlings he would be dealing with. People. Just like himself.

Stretched out on his back in the sun, hands tucked comfortably behind his head, he spotted the unusual sight of a lone traveler wheeling across the sky at very low speed as if looking for something on the ground. All at once Cambian knew. It was Moses and he was looking for *him*. Cambian was about to call out when the wheel suddenly reversed direction and plummeted towards the ground.

Stirring up a dust devil as the wheel uncoiled, Moses landed on his feet, his travel wheel swirling away to nothingness.

Cambian jumped to his feet and raced to greet him. "You're looking pretty good for a 4,000-year-old man!" he grinned, clapping his hands to the man's shoulders in a commonly accepted gesture of affection.

Moses laughed and likewise clapped his own hands to the shoulders of the lean, muscular, 130 pound 5' 5" youth.

"I see you've been spending a lot of time at the beach," Cambian remarked. He could tell because the old man's brown curls were tinged with gold the way they always got when he'd been vacationing at the seaside.

The "old man," his svelte body muscular, his deep brown eyes clear and bright, didn't look as though he'd reached 20 years of age.

Moses nodded and grinned. "Yes. I've been taking a little rest and relaxation at the ocean, thinking about the time the Lord and I parted the Red Sea." He chuckled, "But that's an old story!"

Cambian laughed. These creatures rarely spoke in terms of compartmentalized time. Unconfined by time, they didn't measure it. Simply, there was no time. They were forever. And forever living in the present. How long had he been at the beach? A hundred years? A hundred days? Who was counting? He had stayed until he'd had enough.

"I heard you volunteered for a code-six," Moses said, turning serious, "and I came looking for you." It was traditional for Moses to give a youth who had taken a code-six some fatherly advice before the kid left on the journey.

"That's right, Pops."

"Pops" was a term of affection used by most everyone for the wise and elderly statesman.

A silence fell between them momentarily. Cambian had very straight, shiny black hair, smooth olive-brown skin and deep-brown, almond-shaped eyes. Looking no more than 14 in appearance, his actual age as measured by Earthbound humans was 38, still a baby by anyone's heavenly measure. During the Vietnam war, when just a lad of 14, he'd been savagely raped and murdered by a monster disguised as a soldier.

"Let's walk awhile," Moses said, drawing the boy close with an arm about the shoulders. They turned and strolled alongside the stream. "It's going to be rough down there," he began. Cambian started to say something but Moses shushed him. "Listen. I know it hasn't been that long since you've been away, but *here* one tends to forget what it's like to be contained in a vessel subject to cold, hunger, and pain. And you haven't felt loneliness in what, some 24 years? Now, I don't know the nature of your mission as yet, but walking around down there isn't going to be easy. Are you *sure* you want to do it? The Lord will understand if you have a change of heart after talking with me. I mean, that is part of my job you know."

Cambian nodded. "I know. I want to go. It'll be a great honor to play a key role in America's conversion. And it should be fairly easy as well. After all, they are *my* people."

Moses looked at him sharply. *"Your* people!?"

"Well, I mean, Earthlings. Men. Just like me. And highly sophisticated, with all kinds of equipment for beaming messages. I was discussing it with the Lord this afternoon. We have a very workable plan. I figure it'll be a snap. An easy job with big-ticket credit in return."

Moses laughed lightly. "You ever been to America?"

"I've only seen it from the sky," Cambian admitted.

Again Moses chuckled, advising, "Don't be fooled by appearances, Cambian, it's not going to be as easy as you think."

"I know. I've got a friend on the blue team, O'Rourke, who specializes in monitoring political developments. I'm going to talk to him about it this evening."

"I see," Moses answered thoughtfully, then shrugged. "Well, at least you're approaching this thing sensibly. I mean, research and preparation are everything. After that, if you think you can handle it, go for it."

"Anyway, I've got ten years to prepare," Cambian added. "Touchdown doesn't come until the boy grows up. He's only six now." After a moment he said, "Well, I'd better get started for home. The whole squad will be wondering what's keeping me."

"You want me to fly there with you?" Moses asked as they stopped walking and turned to face one another.

Cambian shook his head. "No, thanks Pops. I feel like walking."

Moses slowly nodded that he understood, raised a hand in farewell and said, "Stand back, then, and I'll be off."

Cambian took two steps back.

"Come see me when you get back from your next mission," Moses called as he started gathering energy about himself, his body beginning to fade as he started dematerializing for the windup.

"Bye!" Cambian called with a wave.

"Bye!" Moses called back, his electromagnetic energy centralized and already turning, a dust devil kicking up as he lifted off and was gone, arcing across the sky in a fiery wheel of light that was him.

CLOUD DROPS

5

PERFECT LOVE

> *But they which shall be accounted worthy to obtain that world, and the resurrection from the dead, neither marry nor are given in marriage.*
>
> *- Luke 20:35*

By the time Cambian made it home, taking a shortcut across the front yard, late afternoon sunshine was streaming through the majestic willow trees and crickets were chirruping madly. His teammates, lounging on the front porch of the mansion they shared, were sipping tall glasses of lemonade and swapping funny stories while waiting for him.

"Hey, gang!" he called with a wave.

"Hey, Cambian!" they called back.

"Where're the kids?" Cambian asked, plopping down on the lowest step with a contented sigh. Propping his right ankle on his left knee, he began slapping dust and tiny bits of gravel from the bottom of his foot.

"Oh, they're around someplace," Michelle, one of Cambian's three girlfriends, answered. "Probably exploring the house."

"Or playing in the pool," someone else put in.

James, caught in a crossfire at the age of 15 in the streets of Belfast during a brief eruption of violence in the

ongoing civil war, asked, "Did you get the code-six assignment?"

"I sure did," Cambian replied as he reversed position
and started slapping his left foot.

"We're proud of you, Cambian," someone else said.

"When you touching down?" another asked.

"Oh, it won't be for quite a few years, yet," Cambian
answered, "but we've got a lot of work to do before that
happens."

*   *   *

Although anyone who wanted could have a private residence all to himself, no one had ever heard of anyone on
Universe Center so choosing, for these were communal
creatures by nature.

As with everything else, nighttime rituals were a plea-
surable communal experience. Then they would lie down
together in groups of at least two and as many as five or six.
Although sexless they were by no means lovemaking-less,
the sheer intensity and longevity of which would make
Earthling sex seem like a mere spurt in the pan by compar-
ison. Designed solely to enhance intimacy and bring
physical pleasure rather than as a means of procreation,
lovers would transform into their aural-electrical bodies and
"spark" each other in an intermingling that could involve
any number of partners. And lovemaking usually lasted for
hours, until having achieved a pleasant euphoria, lovers
drifted into "dreamphase," in many respects the equivalent
of sleep. Though not a necessity, dreamphase was a pleasant, intimate interlude between lovemaking and the
beginning of the day's activities.

Unpossessive by nature and lacking feelings of jealousy
or the need to dominate another tended to preclude any and

all problems Earthlings might encounter under similar circumstances. Even so, naturally, every person had their favorites. Or more commonly, group of favorites. Still, whom one chose to lie beside could be based on any number of insignificant variables such as a mutual interest in a certain sport, which would be discussed the whole night long, or who liked whose singing, or maybe to hear another chapter of an ongoing story someone was telling. And it was nothing to "wake" another in the middle of the night just to tell an especially good joke suddenly remembered.

And no one was left out. If one wanted to crawl in with two or three others they would just move over and make room, for everyone was young and strong and beautiful and burned hot with the fire of God's love.

As to how many rescue teams actually existed only God knew, their journeys and duties being as varied and large in scope as the universe itself. Among the various squads on Earth duty, though, was a good-natured rivalry, each squad wearing a "uniform" consisting of nothing more than a pair of light cotton shorts. And normally the shorts were only worn as a matter of custom when traveling or greeting guests. Otherwise, they were just as likely to be forgotten as not.

Cambian's team had gray shorts with a little blue emblem of three interlocking rings on the right hip. Other teams had green shorts or red or yellow or blue, with their own emblems on the hip and made of the same cotton material.

As it was customary for an incoming team to stop and party with an outgoing team, on this particular evening Cambian and his 17 companions were all sitting in a huge circle on the front lawn of their 42-room mansion waiting for the incoming blue team to arrive.

Georgia, a gorgeous green-eyed lass with flaming red hair, was suggesting breaking out the instruments when another pointed skyward, calling, "Look, here they come!"

Everyone looked up to watch the blue team come in.

Their women having returned in groups of two or three throughout the course of the mission, at this point all that remained of the 18 members of the blue team were the five men.

They came arcing across the sky from out of the eternal night of deep space, five fiery-bluish wheels of light interlinked in the usual disc of travelers holding hands. Even as they arrived from out of the west, a much larger disc appeared from out of the east, its 13 fiery wheels interlinked in the same manner, but with a difference. Every wheel of the larger disc glowed with a bright orange "eye" at its center. It was the women of the blue team arriving from their own home base on Universe Center 30 miles to the east, and they were carrying their "newborns," as the most recently rescued were referred to.

Overhead, the two discs hovered a few feet apart for a moment, then broke into a shower of sparks that dropped glittering to the ground where O'Rourke and his crew uncoiled with a *snap!* and landed on their feet.

*   *   *

The members of the various squadrons were always top-heavy with women because, simply put, there were more women in heaven than men, as so many men, traditionally, were lost in the battle between good and evil. Such was the lure of power and money on Earth. And war.

Motivation for engaging in warfare was everything, and fear of imprisonment was not an acceptable motive. Nor was passion, patriotism, hatred of a particular political system, race, or religion, no matter how carefully disguised as something else. In short, all soldiers were required to seek the blessing (permission) of the Lord before going into battle. Those who went without the Lord's blessing went into combat not as soldiers, but as murderers in disfavor with God. And stating that one had only done as one had been told played no better before the Tribunal of God than it had at the trials of Nuremberg after World War Two.

Even had there not been a shortage of males, the rescue squads on Earth duty would have been top-heavy with women because of the primary nature of the mission, which was to bring in the "children"—victims of sudden death who, for whatever reason, had no relatives, lovers, or friends standing by to greet them on their ascent to the afterworld. For it was the women who dropped from the "spacecraft" and plummeted to Earth in fighter squadrons of two or three to intercept the "children" as, with fearful clumsiness, they first left their "Earth Units" to tumble heavenward stricken with terror of the unknown. Still "babies" so to speak, they lacked the ability to roil-up their energies and take a focused direction on their own.

Taking the "children" inside themselves (literally to the center of the wheel—the center of their Being), it was for the women to bear children again. But without the pain, the weight, morning sickness or a desire for pickles and ice cream. Without the stress of mounting hospital bills, dirty diapers or a squalling, helpless child. Without the emptiness of wondering where the father was, or if he would ever be there at all to offer any kind of support.

Bearing one of these had other pleasures as well. To see their terror-stricken faces change to innocent wide-eyed wonder at the first encounter. To experience the "child's" first sharing of the nurturing spirit. To hear his or her excited laughter at a brief game of hide-and-seek among the clouds with a thundering F-15 jet-fighter, or to see their expressions as they stand upon the moon for the first time to gaze down upon the blue orb of Earth. Then, for the women and their "newborns" the long journey home would begin, while the rest of the rescue squad traveled on with a wave (or a wobble) goodbye. And once carried, with an eternity to share, the child would never forget her, the depths of their intimacy knowing no bounds. Perfect love.

Thus would a team make its way across the sky, dropping a squad here or there as it went and growing progressively smaller along the way, until all the women of the team were on their way home with their precious cargos.

The responsibilities of the men of a given team were of a more Earthbound and less joyous nature. Most who were liberated from the Earth rarely desired to return, and in fact were prohibited from appearing physically, or even revealing their existence.

More than prohibited, actually. There was a stopgap measure designed into their operating systems triggered by Earth's atmosphere and gravitational rating that prevented them from materializing. If they even tried a paralytic reaction would set in and they would float helplessly and invisibly into the sky to be reactivated later by their teammates on the way out.

The frustrating part came when the Elite wanted to help an Earthling in trouble. Invisible and without physical presence, they had a few tricks at their disposal but their ability to intervene was extremely limited.

Another task assigned them, and one more satisfying, was chasing off "Other Ones," lost souls relegated by their own weaknesses to the vicinity between the Earth and moon, who didn't have enough energy to light a spark, let alone materialize. Power-wise, Other Ones were like little kids in paddleboats on a pond at the zoo, the Elite, in

1200-horsepower cigarette boats on the Great Lakes. Inclined to congregate around world leaders, or even persons of lesser importance, Other Ones, through "channeling" (a form of possession), delighted in guiding Earthlings into disasters. In the past, in fact, whole nations had thus been guided straight into fiery hell, and would have dragged the rest of the world down with them if they'd had the means. (Germany, 1939 - 1945.)

*   *   *

After the blue team greeted their hosts and dropped to the grass among them, Cambian took the opportunity to stand and ask what everyone would like for dinner.

"Steak and lobster!" someone called out, which was enthusiastically seconded by members of both teams.

"Then steak and lobster it is!" Cambian proclaimed, "but first, to the baths!"

And then everyone was swarming through the house to the fountains and pools at the rear, kicking off their shorts as they went and hollering things like, "Last one in's a rotten egg!" Or, "So-and-so wears army boots on his ears!" Within seconds all 36 of them, plus the children, were running naked through the waterfalls and splashing in the pool.

After a solid hour of this frantic play, everyone luxuriantly exhausted, they left the water and stretched out on big flat rocks still warm from the sun earlier.

Cambian lay down beside O'Rourke, the political scientist, and Debbie, a vivacious golden-haired lass with blue-green eyes that changed with her moods. Of Cambian's three girlfriends she was undoubtedly his favorite. After they rested a moment, the three of them close together on their stomachs, their arms about each other's shoulders generating a cozy warmth, Cambian asked softly, "Anything new down there, O'Rourke?"

"The same," O'Rourke answered after a pause. "Despite the easing of international tensions, fear and paranoia in America still seem on the rise." He hesitated. "They seem intent on abandoning the very ideals that held such a promising example to the rest of the world. Many want to censor music...."

"Censor *music?*" Cambian was shocked. America had always been the bastion of free speech.

"A bunch of old politicos' wives are flapping their lips about protecting children, but take it from an old scientist, they're really afraid their own decadence and corruption will find them out—unless they can dampen free speech. And that starts with artistic expression.

"And the integrity of the justice system is so compromised that as often as not a guilty person goes free while an innocent one is convicted. We've recorded instances of police officers pulling the trigger for mobsters, and kids shooting other kids for their shoes or jacket. At the same time," O'Rourke paused to catch his breath, "out of fear and media-generated hysteria more and more people are willing to relinquish their civil rights. And sexual repression is making a big comeback which undoubtedly will create a whole new generation of weirdo sex-monsters, inviting even further repression and more monsters."

"I wonder when they start burning the books?" Debbie commented cynically.

"I wonder when they start burning the people!" O'Rourke retorted.

For the second time since making the decision Cambian was beginning to get a little apprehensive about "touching down." Maybe Moses had been right. Maybe this wasn't going to be as easy as he thought.

When everyone was dry and warm Cambian and his two companions sat up, Cambian calling out, "Everyone ready to hit the table?"

Everyone was, and since no one felt like cooking they all joined hands and trooped into the house simply willing the feast, sizzling steaks, broiled lobster, and several buttered vegetable dishes, into existence.

After dinner and the congratulatory speeches regarding Cambian's decision to walk the Earth, and with the guests beginning to drift outside, others decided to clean up the dishes and take down the tables just for the fun of it. Setting up an assembly line, soon dishes were flying through the air like frisbees as they were tossed from person to person to the kitchen.

In the steamy hot kitchen everything was a furious whirlwind of clattering dishes being washed, dried, and stacked in the cupboards in the same rapid-fire fashion. The object of the "game," of course, was to see how fast the mission could be completed without any dishes getting broken.

Outside, the air was filled with the laughter of children playing catch-and-tag among the clouds, while the band was setting up in the ballroom and Cambian and his girls were stocking two bars at either end of the porch with soda and various fruit coolers.

Needless to say the party was a huge success, but by midnight the blue team, weary from their most recent mission, began saying their goodbyes, and by 12:15 a.m. they were gathered in a huge circle on the front lawn. Everyone gave a last wave and then the blue team collectively roiled-up their energies and lifted off for home.

CLOUD DROPS

6

THE GREAT DEBATE

> *In my father's house are many mansions....*
> *- JOHN 14:2*

When Cambian awoke buried beneath the warmth of Debbie, Natalie, and Michelle, the first thing that popped into his head was that he'd forgotten to tell anyone he was supposed to appear before the House of Kings first thing in the morning. Jesus was going to present the plan and Cambian was the code-six volunteer. He was supposed to be there.

The shock of this realization electrified everyone and they sprang awake exclaiming in unison, "What's wrong?"

"I've got an appointment at the House of Kings this morning," Cambian said.

The girls rolled out of bed in three different directions, Debbie holding up his gray cottons, "And you're late, I can tell!"

"Only if they're waiting for me," Cambian replied, springing out of bed and into his shorts in one motion. "I'll be back before midday." Roiling-up, he zipped through the wall and was gone.

The House of Kings was so-named as a gathering place of debate among the universe's great personalities and was not exclusive of females. In fact anyone could attend (provided the issue at hand concerned their native planet) to put forth an opinion or to simply vote on a particular issue, the capacity of the great hall simply expanding or contracting as needs required.

At the moment Jesus was pacing the floor before the assembly, his white, gold-embroidered robes flowing, as Siddhartha Gautoma (the Buddha) spoke in a quiet, even tone, "Pat Patterson is a loud, clanging bell of discontent among the people, suffering from the same superiority complex that his kind have always suffered from, and spreading diversity and calamity among the people on a worldwide scale at a time when international relations have never been better. Should we, then, pursue his son in the hope that *he* will join us in our quest for peace?"

Straining against the armrests of his chair, Malcolm X could barely contain himself waiting for the Buddha to conclude. When the great religious leader finally gathered his robes about himself and relinquished the floor, Malcolm found his feet, loudly proclaiming, "Pat Patterson is a racist! You're going to use *him?*"

Waving him back to his seat, Jesus' tone was reassuring. "Now just chill out, Malcolm, Patterson has blacks on his show."

"Tokens!" Malcolm thundered, "Tokens!"

"Well that may or may not be. In any case, if we win him over through his son, or even if we only win over his son, heir apparent, what does it matter? *We'll* be in the driver's seat. I mean, believe you me, I have a few things to say to that man myself. Imagine him blaming *me* for people being trapped in cycles of poverty. As if I created the system that generates ghettos and leaves people homeless. But

don't you worry, before this is all over we're going to tell
him a thing or two!"

Looking a little unsure, Malcolm reluctantly took his
seat even as Mohammed, the father of Islam, rose. "Sir,
truly I am baffled. Here is a man who daily speaks against
my people. Indeed, psychologically prepares his own for
war with Moslems through inflammatory speeches, having
said over and over again on television that the day will
come when his people will have to take up arms against my
people. That eventually it's either going to be the Christians
or the Moslems who will rule the world. To what purpose
would we deal with one like this?"

Jesus calmly waved Mohammed down too, saying reassuringly, "Come now, Mohammed, *I'm* not a Christian." At
that the assembly burst out laughing. After the laughter subsided, Jesus continued, "Let me assure you my brother, any
friend of yours is a friend of mine."

This brought the entire assembly to its feet applauding.
When it had grown quiet and everyone returned to their
seats, Mahatma Gandhi, the greatest modern spiritual leader
of Hinduism, (and present representative, as the ancient
founders of some 3,000 years ago were already hard at work
on a distant world planting the seeds of God-consciousness
among a race of brutes that had barely discovered fire),
cried from his seat, "And what about us? He calls *us* responsible for the proliferation of Satanism!"

To which John Lennon called out, "Don't let that ruffle
your feathers, son, you're only in with the rest of them
Moslems and Buddhists!"

Again the assembly burst into laughter and applause,
while Linda McCartney, who happened to be sitting next to
George Harrison and Lennon, leaned close with an amused
smile and whispered, "I wish I'd eaten my meat."

With a chuckle, Harrison remarked, "It didn't take me

so long to see My Sweet Lord after all, eh?'"

"Does that fall under 'watch out what you pray for, you might get it?'" Lennon snickered.

Mother Teresa, sitting in the row below with Geronimo, Janis Joplin, and Pancho Villa, leaned forward and spoke softly into the ear of Diana, Princess of Wales, "The only ones responsible for the proliferation of Satanism are Satan and those who reject God."

Lennon couldn't help himself and quipped, "If Diana is the Princess of Wales, who's the Princess of Tuna?"

The ruckus was still going on when Cambian landed on the front lawn outside, straightened his shorts, ran across the dew-damp grass, up the stone steps gritty against his bare feet, pulled open one of the heavy brass doors and went inside.

As the laughter and applause subsided, Jesus, glancing at the boy, turned back to the assembly and announced, "And now I'd like to introduce the young man who has volunteered to see the mission through." Turning to Cambian, he said, "Come out here, son."

Cambian shyly stepped into the midst of the forum and stopped beside Jesus, who drew him close with an arm about the shoulders. "This, my friends, is Cambian, our code-six volunteer."

The assembly applauded enthusiastically. Afterwards Mohammed spoke first. "Did you establish contact with the youth, Cambian?"

"Yes sir, I did," Cambian replied.

"And?"

"He was very receptive, sir. We established an immediate rapport."

"And don't forget, ladies and gentlemen," Jesus interjected, "this is a long-range plan. Cambian and his teammates are going to work with the lad over the next ten years, putting forth our ideas telepathically from the air a little at a time while watching to see how he responds—if he'll argue our case even at risk to his Earthly throne. The one his father built for him. Only then, and only if necessary, will Cambian actually touch down. So you see, it's a perfectly safe and workable plan. If at any time we decide we've targeted the wrong individual we can simply pull out and dissolve the program with no harm done to anyone. If it doesn't work out, well, we won't necessarily be any better off, but we won't be any worse off either." Jesus paused and looked around the assembly. "Any questions?"

A brief murmur arose as people consulted with their neighbors. When silence once again prevailed, Jesus said, "Then I move to incorporate the 'Patterson Plan' into our long-range operations. All in favor say 'aye.'"

The assembly responded with one loud "Aye!"

"All against signify with 'nay.'"

Not one "Nay" was heard.

"Then it's unanimous," Jesus said in conclusion. Turning to Cambian he added, "Well, I guess you're on."

CLOUD DROPS

7

LIFE GOES ON

> *And Jesus saith unto them, Yea: have ye never read, Out of the mouth of babes and sucklings thou hast perfected praise?*
> *- MATTHEW 21:16*

The loud, coarse buzzing of the alarm clock suddenly shattered the morning quietude. Ten-year-old Ledyard Patterson, still groggy with sleep, blindly groped for the clock on the bedside table and snapped it off. Sitting up, he dug at an eye with the heel of one hand and looked around the room. Had they come again last night while he was sleeping? Were they, whoever "they" were, putting thoughts in his head during the night through some sort of telepathy? Or had his experience by the walnut tree with the Invisible Ones four years previously just been a dream? Or was he just crazy with loneliness?

Heaving a sigh of resignation, Ledyard put these thoughts behind him and rolled out of bed. He had another day to face. And for him being in the fifth grade was no picnic. He made a beeline for the bathroom, stopped before the sink and turned on the water.

Ledyard Patterson hated being chauffeured to school in the family's Cadillac stretch limo, one of a stable of ·

expensive cars kept for his parents' personal use. Of course he would have hated it just as much in the family's Rolls Royce. In fact he hated being chauffeured at all. The grammar school, provided for the children of the Christian Condensed Ministry's 247 employees and local supporters, was only ten blocks away. While the other kids who lived off campus arrived in typical yellow school busses, and the ones who lived on the 6,000-acre campus usually walked, he pulled up in this big stretch limo with the family's bodyguard/chauffeur at the wheel. Thus he always stood out, apart, the butt of endless razzing by his classmates. It had been that way from day one, the others assuming he was a stuck-up arrogant little brat flaunting his wealth and famous background. And at the tender age of ten kids can be merciless.

Ledyard long ago gave up efforts to be allowed to walk to school. His father didn't seem to understand. The last time Ledyard brought up the subject, in September when school began, his father had been adamant. Appearances must be kept up. After all, he was the son of a rich and famous minister, which made *him,* in effect, famous too, and Ledyard would just have to get used to it.

More importantly, though, were matters of security to consider. Although there were two guards at the front gate and several in patrol cars, the campus was just too big. A determined intruder could easily slip in. Besides, his father assured him, with time, as the other kids got to know him and they all matured together they would see that he was just another kid like them. From a rich and famous family maybe, but deep inside just another kid growing up in unusual circumstances.

Washed and scrubbed and standing before the bureau mirror in his bedroom, Ledyard was getting dressed in the obligatory school uniform of navy-blue trousers, white shirt with burgundy tie, and navy-blue blazer with the Christian Condensed crest on the left breast pocket. For the girls it was blue plaid skirts, white blouses, and blue-knit cardigan sweaters, also sporting the Christian Condensed crest. He was combing his hair when his father's voice, sounding thin and metallic through the speaker, called over the mansion's intercom system, "Hurry up, boy, or you're goin' to be late."

He heard the *click* and hollow hum that told him his father was now monitoring—waiting for a response. "Okay," Ledyard said loudly so the mic in the wall unit on the far side of the room would pick up his reply. "Be right there."

He heard the machine click off, tossed the brush on the dresser, grabbed his books, hurried from the room, down the hall, and took the backstairs down to the kitchen where his mother and father were already having breakfast.

*   *   *

"When will those people downtown get it through their thick heads? We're not a shelter for the homeless, we're a Bible college and television ministry!" Pat Patterson fumed to his wife as he sat in the breakfast nook stirring his coffee.

At 6' 1" the pleasant-faced, ruddy-cheeked 35-year-old televangelist had perfect white teeth, a finely shaped nose, clear blue eyes and a wide, boyish smile. He could have been a Hollywood movie star. He was the number one talk show host of televised religious programming, darling of the right wing fundamentalist movement and a growing influence throughout the country.

"I think," Brenda May Patterson began contemplatively, "that maybe they're hopin' if they call here often enough we'll donate money to their toady little shelter." She paused as Elly, their black maid, set a saucer of toast before each of them.

"Well they aren't gonna get it!" the reverend declared, spreading strawberry jam on his toast. "If those people would give their hearts to Jesus they wouldn't be livin' in the streets! The fact that they're homeless is evidence enough they've rejected Christ. Once a body done that, well, t'ain't much I can do for 'em 'cept teach the truth a Jesus. And that's where *my* responsibility ends!"

"That certainly is the truth," Brenda May huffed. "Why, if they'd just sow one seed gift of five dollars," she snapped her fingers, "their situation would change overnight." Both looked up as their son came in.

"But what if they don't have five dollars, mamma?" their son asked, stopping just inside the door.

"Well darlin', then they aren't right with Jesus. The Lord don't let *his* go without!"

Wiping crumbs from the counter, Elly asked over her shoulder, "What'll it be dis mornin', Ledyard?"

"Cereal."

"Here, sit down boy," his father said, pulling a chair out. "And open your mouth when you talk and pick up your feet when you walk."

Setting his books on the far end as he made his way around the table, Ledyard slid into the chair at the right of his father and directly across from his mother.

Brenda May Patterson was the perfect match to her husband; thin, attractive, tall, intelligent, with light brown hair and blue eyes just like his. Except for her short little pug nose and pouty lips they could have been siblings. "Honey, your tie's crooked," she said to her son.

Ledyard adjusted his tie as Elly set a bowl of cereal and a carton of milk before him. "There. How's that?" he asked.

"Perfect, darlin'," his mother smiled.

Pulling the bowl closer, Ledyard looked to either side and called out, "Elly, you forgot my spoon!"

"Oh! Sorry, child," she apologized, getting a spoon from the silverware drawer and bringing it to him.

"Thanks." Ledyard would have been the spitting image of his father, tall, blond, blue, except for the cute little button nose and full lips he inherited from his mother. Pouring milk on his Cocoa-Puffs, Ledyard looked up at his father. "Daddy?"

"What, son?"

"What's it sound like when God talks to you?"

"It don't *sound* like nothin', Ledyard. God speaks quiet to my heart."

"But how do you know it's God talkin' and not just you sort of talkin' to yourself?"

Pat Patterson frowned, answering, "Because I know my master's voice."

"But you said you don't hear his voice, daddy."

Eyeing his son gravely, the reverend set his toast down. "Are you sassin' me, boy?"

"No sir," Ledyard quickly responded. "But sometimes I think God's talkin' to me, too, but it seems like it's comin' to my *head.*"

"God touches men's hearts, boy," the Texas preacher said firmly. "If somethin's talkin' to your mind then it surely t'ain't God."

"Then what is it, daddy? Angels?"

"Angels!" his father scoffed. "Now why would an angel want to talk to a young'n like you?"

Ledyard shrugged, spooning cereal. "I don't rightly know. In the Old Testament God spoke to Samuel when *he* was just a young'n, though."

The reverend sighed, his patience wearing thin. "Now look, boy, God, angels, whatever, they speak to men's hearts, not their heads. If you're feelin' right sure somethin's speakin' to your mind," he shook his head, "t'ain't likely to be God. I suggest that the next time it happens you just call on the name a Jesus and cast that evil spirit out."

Ledyard nodded, risking further comment. "But it didn't seem evil, daddy."

"Son, the Bible says even Satan can appear as an angel of light. And it sounds to me like you have a whole host of evil spirits messin' with your mind. So you just do like I told you and cast that evil spirit out the next time it comes 'round. Now finish your cereal and get movin'. I'm sure Mr. Granger is already out front awaitin' on you."

*   *   *

Smartly dressed in a navy-blue uniform with gleaming brass buttons and a cap, John Granger, Ledyard's bodyguard/chauffeur, was just getting out of the idling limousine in the bricked circular drive when Ledyard came out the front door.

Nodding his "Good mornin', Mr. Granger," Ledyard crossed the huge front porch with its four massive columns towering three stories high, trundled down the five broad stone steps and disappeared inside the car as the chauffeur sprang-to and opened the door, likewise nodding his own cheerful, "Good mornin', Mr. Patterson."

Ledyard's relationship with his bodyguard/chauffeur was rather cordial if formal. Over the last two years, though, Ledyard had made up his mind that John Granger was a big no-hitter. Especially since the man claimed to have gained his martial arts expertise under the tutelage of Chuck Norris before Norris had become a big movie star. He had even offered to introduce Ledyard to him someday.

Of course someday never came, and although Granger was trim and solidly built at 30 years of age, Ledyard rarely saw him working out at the Christian Condensed Health Club, and never saw him practicing his martial arts skills, even though Ledyard had repeatedly asked for a demonstration. Granger always countered with some lame excuse like a muscle being pulled or a toe stubbed. Ledyard did know that Granger carried a small pistol tucked beneath the left armpit of his jacket.

And the man was so rigid! Simply put, Ledyard could not get him to bend an inch either way of his expressed orders. Like at the very beginning of the year when Ledyard asked to be let out a block from school so he could walk and take a little morning sunshine.

"No way," Granger had replied, "my orders are to put you off at the front door and that's what I'm going to do." Period.

And Granger followed him everywhere, day in and day out. Not that Ledyard had very many playmates to run off with and do the things that boys do in secret at that age. But he couldn't even sit in the backyard beneath the walnut tree, which he often liked to do. To wait. To contemplate. To pray. With the vague notion that maybe his "Invisible Friends," if they really existed at all, would return. Not without feeling Granger's eyes on him.

Thus he had the discomforting sense of *always* being watched. And he was. Whether at the pool, the tennis courts, or the private bowling alley in the basement, Granger was there. It seemed to intensify Ledyard's sense of loneliness, for although he was never alone, he was always lonely. And there was no escaping it as some might by cultivating a taste for solitude, because even *that* doggedly escaped him—in the form of the ever watchful Granger.

Except for four days at the end of every month. Then, like clockwork Granger would disappear. Always the last week of the month. And always Sunday nights through Wednesdays. For a long time Ledyard had no idea where Granger went, either. And when he asked his father he was simply told that it was none of his business.

Once, though, when Granger was in the shower just before leaving on one of his trips, Ledyard crept into the man's suite of rooms on the mansion's third floor and discovered a commercial airline ticket for Switzerland lying on the bed. It struck the boy as odd, considering that the ministry had two of its own corporate jets. Ledyard knew they could make trans-Atlantic flights because he had gone to Europe on one with his mother and father. Another thing Ledyard noticed—the airline ticket had been paid for in cash.

As Granger wheeled the stretch limo up the drive and stopped before the front doors of the school, he looked at Ledyard in the rearview mirror and said the same thing he had said every morning for the last two years, "Then we'll see you here at 3:30 this afternoon?"

"Yes sir," Ledyard replied, pulling at the door handle and wishing just once he could get out by himself. But it was always locked. Security.

Granger hit the unlock button, sprang from the car, drew Ledyard's door open and stood aside, chirping, "Good day, sir!"

"Good day," Ledyard said without much enthusiasm, pulling his books after him as he slid off the seat and got out.

Then Granger would stand there and watch until he was safely inside the school. That was the pathetic part. He couldn't even stand outside and mill about with the others until the bell rang. At least not without having that cursed chauffeur standing there beside that cursed limousine watching his every cursed move.

Ledyard walked up the broad concrete sidewalk to the plateglass doors of the modernish, yellow-brick grammar school and disappeared inside without looking back.

Inside, he plopped down on the long, low bench in the hall outside the principal's office where unruly kids were sent to wait for a session with the stern disciplinarian. To pass the time until the bell rang summoning the other kids, he opened his American History book and browsed through the part about the Puritans burning the witches.

With a loud clatter of shoes and books, talking and laughter, the herd of six- through 11-year-olds stormed into the building even before the bell stopped ringing, someone shouting above the din, "I wonder what Ledyard did *now* to get in trouble!"

After his last bleating tormentor had passed, Ledyard got to his feet and followed. In homeroom he made his way to his desk, second-to-last aisle from the windows, third seat down, ignoring the usual snide remarks such as, "How come Ledyard's always last?" To which someone would invariably reply, "His limo wouldn't start and he's still learnin' to walk!"

Then the teacher would slap her ruler against her desktop and sharply call, "All right, enough!" And class would begin.

*   *   *

Something unusual happened during recess after lunch. Another fifth-grader, Lonny Anderson, reputedly the toughest kid in school, approached Ledyard at the swing set where the friendless boy usually spent recess alone, sitting at the far end on the last swing, sometimes swinging just as high as he could for the entire 30 minute period. Sometimes just sitting, staring, waiting.

Today Ledyard was sitting. At first he was surprised, then apprehensive as he watched Lonny approach. Most of the other kids stopped what they were doing to watch, too.

Lonny was somehow scruffier than the other kids. Although he wore the same uniform with tie required of all the boys, his suits were always a bit worn, threadbare in some places, and obviously too small—except on that rare occasion when he came walking proudly into school with a new suit, and then it would be too big and loose fitting. His brown hair was on the longish side too—except when he came to school with a new haircut, and then it seemed he'd practically been scalped.

Lonny was also somewhat more streetwise than the other kids. An off-campus student who came to school on the bus, his father was a mail carrier, and they lived on Houston's poorer east side in an older district where a lot of blacks and Mexicans lived.

Ledyard looked down at his shoes as Lonny approached and stopped beside him. "Hey, Ledyard."

Ledyard looked up with a nervous smile. "Hey, Lonny."

Lonny sat down on a swing next to Ledyard. Absently kicking at the sand with the toe of one shoe, he asked, "How come ya ain't swingin' today?"

"Don't know," Ledyard shrugged, "just don't feel like it, I guess."

"Well ya got a lot more practice than me, and I'll bet I can *still* swing higher."

Ledyard eyed the boy for a thoughtful moment before meeting the challenge. "Can't neither."

"Can so," Lonny replied, pushing off.

Pumping furiously, both boys strained against the chains, climbing higher and higher until they were topped-out. For a moment it seemed the contest would become who could hold out the longest, but then Lonny shouted, "Draw?"

"Draw!" Ledyard shouted back.

Immediately both boys relaxed and let the swings slow until they were scuffing their feet to stop.

"Well it was a draw," Ledyard declared defensively.

Lonny shrugged. "Ya got more practice swingin', but I bet I can piss higher!"

The challenge couldn't have come at a better time. Ledyard had decided to go in and take one just before Lonny had come over, then forgot all about it. Now he had to go. Bad. "Bet you can't!" he shot back with a sudden confidence that surprised even him.

"Let's go, then," Lonny said as both boys leapt off their swings and headed for "The Wall."

The Wall was a section of the exterior gymnasium structure, two stories tall and windowless, that jutted out from the rest of the grammar school and provided a shadowy, secluded corner mostly out of view of the schoolyard.

As soon as the boys abandoned their swings and made a beeline for the corner, everyone knew what was up, the playground emptying in the general direction of The Wall. The girls, though, would shyly hang back, watching from the monkey bars. Having never witnessed one of these contests up close, they had learned the nature of the competition as far back as the second grade when one brave feminine soul surreptitiously wandered over to The Wall afterwards to examine the odorous evidence and returned to the rest of the second grade girls with a full report.

Four spots worn in the turf over the years indicated where contestants stood. The boy that shot it highest on The

Wall won. Lining up, Ledyard and Lonny faced The Wall, undid their trousers and shoved them down to their knees. No one ever merely unzipped and shot from the fly, as that narrow opening was too restrictive, preventing the contestant from cranking back and really putting an arc on it, which was key to the whole thing.

As champion pisser Lonny knew a little trick that gave him an advantage. Right before the *"Go!"* signal was called he'd grasp his penis just behind the head and pinch it closed, letting the pressure build before aiming high. It always worked.

Both boys were giving each other the fisheye as someone called out, "Ready! Set! Go!"

Ledyard leaned back and released a powerful stream, hitting The Wall first. But being first was irrelevant. A moment later, sufficient pressure built-up, Lonny let go, inciting an immediate argument among the spectators.

"Lonny's is higher!" someone shouted.

"T'ain't neither!" another boy vehemently countered, "they're exactly the same!"

"It's true," another put in, "check out the mortar line. They both just wet the bottom of the brick."

"Wow!" A sixth-grader exclaimed, "Ledyard tied Lonny! Turn around Ledyard, let's see!"

"Just a second, I'm still pissin'."

Lonny was already done and zipping up when Ledyard turned around and proudly showed off his wanger.

"It don't look that big to me," one boy said.

"T'ain't no bigger than mine," someone else chimed in.

"Awww, he just got lucky," another said.

Then the bell rang and the boys broke up and started across the playground for class.

"That was pretty good, Ledyard," Lonny admitted as they started back. "You're the first one that ever even come close."

Ledyard shrugged, saying modestly, "Guess I'm just a good pisser."

"I can make you an even better pisser," Lonny intoned.

"How?"

Lonny winked and grinned. "Don't worry none, I'll show ya sometime."

"Thanks, Lonny," Ledyard said, for the first time in his life feeling the warm glow of friendship with a peer.

CLOUD DROPS

8

BOYS AT PLAY

Fear came upon me, and trembling, which made all my bones to shake.

Then a spirit passed before my face; the hair of my flesh stood up....
                                - JOB 4:14 - :15

At breakfast the next morning Ledyard was delighted when his father told him he would have to walk home from school that afternoon. Granger had a doctor's appointment, and although his father would normally pick him up from school during Granger's absences, on this afternoon he wouldn't be available. Both he and mother had an important meeting to attend, his father explained, and had neglected to arrange for Ledyard's transport.

Secretly, though, his parents had discussed the situation the night before and decided it was time to start giving the boy a bit more freedom. After all, they didn't want him growing up *totally* dependent or, horror of horrors, becoming a mamma's boy.

"See if you can't get one of your little friends to come home with you, darlin'," his mother suggested.

"That's a good idea," his father added, warning, "but whatever y'all do, come straight home, understand?"

Quelling his excitement, Ledyard quickly nodded, asking, "Can I walk to school too, daddy?"

"No. Mr. Granger will be here this mornin'. And Elly will be here this afternoon. Y'all can play in the pool if you want or bowl or whatever, but you're to stay indoors until we get home. Okay?"

Ledyard nodded, answering solemnly, "Yes, sir."

That morning when the chauffeur let him out at the usual spot, Ledyard didn't immediately go inside the building. He didn't care if Granger stood there until the cows came home, he was going to find Lonny and invite him over. He felt sure the boy would want to. If only his folks would let him.

The bus had just pulled up, its doors standing open, children beginning to disembark when Ledyard stepped out of the limousine and left Granger with a wave.

Standing on the periphery of the group of students milling about, Ledyard anxiously kept his eye on the stream of kids filing off the bus. It would be just his luck that Lonny would pick today to be sick.

But Lonny wasn't sick. He was just the last one off the bus. "Lonny!" Ledyard called with a wave of his arm, "over here!"

Saying, "Later, y'all," to a little group of friends that had gathered around him after he'd gotten off the bus, Lonny made his way through the crowd of students and joined Ledyard.

"Hey, Lonny." Suddenly aware that everyone was probably staring at them, Ledyard added, "Take a walk inside with me?"

With the exception of Ledyard, the students were absolutely forbidden to enter the school before the bell rang. But as Ledyard's companion, staff wouldn't dare say a word to Lonny. All at once aware of the status that being in

Ledyard's company would bring, Lonny readily agreed, saying casually as if they'd been friends for years, "Sure, Led, what's up?"

"I just wanted to ask you somethin'," Ledyard said as they strode to the bank of glass doors and disappeared inside.

Behind them the doors banged shut, echoing loudly in the dark, deserted hallway, the lights yet to be turned on for the day. "Wow!" Lonny whispered, "Ya sure I ain't gonna get in trouble?"

"Nah," Ledyard grinned at him, "you're with me. Anyway, like I was sayin', I get to walk home this afternoon and my folks said I can bring someone with me. Want to?"

Lonny was still nervously glancing around. "Ya sure it's okay?"

"Guarantee it. You can stay for dinner, too."

"But my folks'll be expectin' me home on the bus this afternoon."

"That's why we're in *here*," Ledyard explained. "So you can call and ask. And you don't have to worry none how you'll get home 'cause my daddy'll just have someone drive you."

Lonny eyed him suspiciously for a moment. "Ya sure 'bout this?"

"Course I'm sure."

Lonny shrugged. "Okay."

"Why don't you call right now so everything'll be set?" Ledyard suggested, knowing full well he'd be fidgety all day if he didn't know whether or not Lonny was coming home with him.

"Where do I call from?"

"Follow me," Ledyard answered, crossing the hall to the front office door.

"In *there?*" Lonny asked incredulously.

Ledyard laughed and pulled the door open, saying, "Don't forget, Lonny, my daddy *owns* this school. Come on," he motioned with his head.

"Okay," Lonny said, following his privileged friend into the office.

Lonny froze just inside the door. "Somebody's here!" he whispered harshly, "the lights are on!"

"So what?" Ledyard said as he made his way around the front counter and stopped at one of several work stations for the secretaries. Along either wall were doors leading to the offices of the various administrators, and two staff rest rooms, one marked "Women," the other "Men."

"I sure hope ya know what you're doin'," Lonny said as he came around the counter and joined his friend.

"Okay, what's your number?"

"Here, let me dial it."

"Sure," Ledyard said, handing him the receiver.

Just as Lonny started dialing, the boys heard a toilet flush and a moment later, the click of high heels against tile as the ladies room door squeaked open and a woman stepped out, exclaiming in a startled voice, "Boys! What're you doing?"

Lonny froze with phone in hand. Ledyard turned around. "It's only me, Miss Kneeling. My friend here is supposed to come home with me this afternoon and has to call his folks."

"Oh! Ledyard, it's you!" she smiled her relief. "You boys gave me quite a start."

"Sorry, Miss Kneeling," Ledyard said apologetically.

"That's quite all right, Ledyard, I know it wasn't intentional. Now you boys just get on with making your call. I've got to go and get the lights turned on."

"Thanks, Miss Kneeling!" Ledyard called as the woman left the front office.

Both boys listened briefly to the click-clicking of her
high heels receding down the hall, then turned to making
the call.

Ledyard watched Lonny's face closely for clues as the
boy spoke with his mother. "What'd she say?" he asked the
moment Lonny hung up.

"She said it was okay," Lonny replied with a grin.

"All right!" Ledyard exclaimed, glad he and Lonny
were in the same room when school let out in case the bad-
dest boy in the fifth grade forgot he was supposed to go
home with him.

                    *   *   *

Ledyard couldn't believe his good fortune. For the first
time in his life he was actually walking down a relatively
public street unsupervised. And with a friend. It filled him
with a delicious sense of freedom. And this was only the
beginning, he told himself. As he got older he would face an
ever expanding horizon of freedom. To go where he wanted
when he wanted. To do whatever he wanted without some
guard watching his every move.

Had he noticed his two escorts in the official ministry
patrol car creeping down the street dogging his every step
from the next block over he would have been terribly dis-
appointed.

"It must be fun bein' as rich an' famous as y'all are,"
Lonny commented as they walked along.

"T'ain't the fun y'all think," Ledyard intoned. "Sometimes I feel like I'm livin' in some kind of fancy prison."

As they started up the front steps of the mansion with
its marble pillars towering three stories, Lonny stopped,
craning his neck back to look up. Letting out a long, low
whistle, he exclaimed, "Wow! This is were y'all *live?*"

Ledyard chuckled. "Sure is." Then he proceeded up the steps. "Come on."

Once in the front foyer with its cathedral ceiling, glittering crystal chandelier, and sweeping grand staircase, Ledyard called out loudly, "Elly, I'm home!" With one ear cocked and waiting for a response, he glanced at Lonny.

"Who's Elly?" Lonny asked.

"The maid."

To the right of the foyer was a gargantuan living room with a huge stone fireplace tall enough to walk in. "Hmmm," Ledyard said half to himself, "I wonder where she is? Come on." He led the way into the living room and stopped before an intercom mounted on the wall, pressed the transmit button and spoke into the machine. "Elly, this is Ledyard. Where are you?"

He pushed the listen button. Almost instantly her voice came through the speaker. "I'm in the utility room doin' laundry, child. There be milk in the fridge and cookies on the table for you and yo' frien'."

He let the listen button go and pushed transmit. "Yes, ma'am, don't worry 'bout us." He let the button go and the machine clicked off. Turning to Lonny, he asked, "Feel like havin' a snack?"

Lonny shrugged. "I don't know, do you?"

"I'd say I'm a little hungry. Come on."

Ledyard led the way back through the foyer, another immense living room, a formal dining room, and through a swinging door that led into a kitchen.

"This is the kitchen?" Lonny asked in surprise. It looked like the industrial-style kitchen one might find in a major restaurant.

"This is *one* kitchen," Ledyard said, "where the servants normally eat and prepare meals for big formal dinner parties and such, but it's not the one *we* use."

There was a big black eight-burner, four-oven stove along the back wall. In the center of the room an island of stainless steel counter had two sinks and an array of pots, fry pans, and utensils hanging overhead. Other accouterments included an assembly line style dish washing machine, gleaming walk-in coolers with massive, bank-vault-sized doors, and at the far end, a small enamel four-place table where the help ate.

"Come on," Ledyard said, leading the way through the room and out another swinging door at the far end, which brought them into a highly modern if more conventional kitchen. "This is the one *we* use."

He opened the refrigerator, removed a carton of milk, grabbed two glasses from an overhead cabinet and went to the breakfast nook off to one side. Lonny joined him at the table in the little alcove of greenhouse glass crawling with ivy and hanging plants that filtered sunlight and offered a measure of privacy. Filling their glasses, Ledyard handed one to Lonny, pulled the plate of chocolate chip cookies to within easy reach and removed the brushed aluminum lid.

"This is some house y'all have here," Lonny commented, reaching for a cookie. "Three floors!"

Ledyard shrugged. "We only ever use two floors. The third is where the servants live and our extra stuff is stored."

Elly came in just as the boys were finishing their milk and cookies. "So, what you boys plannin' dis afternoon?"

Ledyard twisted around in his chair. "Elly, this here's Lonny. Lonny, this here's the maid, Elly."

"Hi," Lonny said, turning to her.

"Good afternoon, Mr. Lonny," Elly said with a nod. "Now the way I understands it, you boys are not to leave the house, an' I got a lot ta do dis afternoon and don' be needin' y'all underfoot, neither."

"No, ma'am," Ledyard replied. "We'll probably be down by the pool or bowlin' or somethin'."

"That's good. I be here an' there if y'all needs anything," she said, then turned and scurried off through the swinging door into the industrial kitchen.

Turning to his friend, Ledyard asked, "Y'all ready for the grand tour or what?"

Lonny nodded. "I sure am."

"Well come on then," Ledyard said, shoving his chair back and leading the way out of the kitchen via a narrow, thickly carpeted passageway just behind the breakfast nook.

"That's the back stairway that leads to the second and third floors," Ledyard said as they passed the staircase and stopped at a door just beyond. "And this'll take us down to the entertainment center." He pulled the door open and led the way down thickly carpeted stairs that twisted around in a tight spiral, little night-lights recessed into the wall at each step. At the bottom was a vast dark room, the dimensions of which Lonny could only sense in the dimness.

Feeling along the wall to his immediate right, Ledyard quickly snapped on four toggle switches. Banks of circular, recessed ceiling lights that seemed to stretch to infinity instantly illuminated the huge room.

"W-Wow!" Lonny sputtered in amazement as he stumbled into the room on Ledyard's heels. It was the size of a small town bowling alley he'd once been in with his father. To the left were the men's and Ladie's rooms. To the right, a bench with a bank of small rectangular lockers for storing shoes and personal effects.

Farther into the room, stretching away to the left, were groups of tables and chairs where spectators could lounge, a three-tiered rack of bowling balls, and six automated bowling lanes. On the right was a substantial bar, the front of which was diamond-tufted, silver studded leather with 12 matching bar chairs. Just beyond the cocktail lounge was the snack bar, a brightly-striped awning defining the area, with a sign above reading "snacks." The game room at the extreme far end had three walls lined with pinball and video machines, and a pool table in the center.

Ledyard turned to his friend. "This here's my play-room."

Lonny's jaw dropped. "Some playroom!"

"Well, t'ain't really *my* playroom," Ledyard admitted with a grin.

"But it's here if ya need it, huh?" Lonny put in.

"Yeah, somethin' like that." He paused as his friend gazed around the room, then said, "But I don't feel like messin' with all this, do you?"

"Uh-uh," Lonny said, shaking his head in stupefied wonder.

"I'd rather go swimmin'," Ledyard quickly added. "Besides, ya haven't seen the pool yet. Let's go." He turned and headed for the exit.

"But I h'ain't got a swimsuit," Lonny said, his head spinning as he hurriedly followed.

"That's all right," Ledyard said over his shoulder, "you can use one of mine. I got a whole drawer full."

"Sure, whatever you say."

Ledyard paused at the foot of the stairs, snapped off the lights, then turned and bounded up.

"This is *your* room?" Lonny asked in disbelief as they entered Ledyard's bedroom.

"Course it is."

Lonny gazed at the stack of stereo equipment, the TV, phone, desk, computer. He crossed the room and opened a door. "What's in here?"

"Bathroom."

From the bathroom came the muffled echo of Lonny's exclamation. "What's this!?"

With a sigh Ledyard abandoned digging through his dresser and went to the bathroom. He was getting bored with this. "It's a jacuzzi," he replied as if everyone had one in their room.

"And this?" Lonny asked, reaching for an opaque glass door.

"Shower."

"Oh."

"You done now?" Ledyard asked, straining to quell the impatience creeping into his voice.

"Sorry."

"Come on, let's get us some swimsuits."

The boys returned to the bedroom where Ledyard dug out a sleek black suit with silver racing stripes and held it up. "This okay?"

"Yeah, sure."

Ledyard tossed it to him and selected a red one with yellow racing stripes for himself.

When Lonny started pulling his tie loose, Ledyard stopped him. "What're ya doin'?"

Lonny froze, staring at him. "Changin'."

"We don't change *here*, we change in the locker room. What're ya gonna do, walk through the whole house in your swimmin' suit?"

"Oh. Sorry."

About to charge off again, Ledyard suddenly stopped and turned to his new friend. "Wait a minute."

"What?" Lonny asked edgily.

"I uh, never brought a friend home before. Guess I'm feelin' a little skittish, like a horse with a new rider."

Lonny nodded. "Yeah. I know what you mean."

"Okay?"

Breathing easier, Lonny smiled. "Yeah, okay."

"Good," Ledyard grinned at him. "Wanna see the pool?"

"Yeah!"

They returned as they had come, by way of the thickly carpeted backstairs. But this time they continued on, past his father's den and various guest rooms and into an elegantly appointed and quietly cavernous room of oak beams and heavy dark paneling nicely set off by rich, forest-green carpet. In the center of the room was a pool table.

"*Another* pool table!" Lonny exclaimed.

"This is the recreation room," Ledyard answered.

Grouped around a tall stone fireplace at the far end were several brown leather easy chairs and a sofa. Before the sofa was a long, low cocktail table of dark wood, the center of which housed a wedge-shaped electronic control console for the video and stereo equipment. A high-density large-screen TV stared blankly from the upper right corner and had huge speakers recessed into the walls at various strategic points around the room.

Off the recreation room was an additional wing of glass, stone, and massive wood ceiling beams that housed a swimming pool, hot tub, sauna, and a workout area defined by a waist-high wall that contained a universal gym, free weights, a treadmill, and two stationary bicycles. Beyond that, two doors led to the men's and women's locker rooms.

In the locker room both boys scrambled into their swimsuits, raced out to the pool and dived in. Bursting to the surface, Lonny joyously cried, "It's so warm!"

"That's because it's heated."

They spit water at one another, which erupted into a fierce water fight. They wrestled. They raced from one end of the pool to the other, saw who could swim the farthest underwater on a single breath, and who could make the biggest cannonball splash. Who could spring the highest off the diving board and who could do the cruelest belly-flop. At last exhausted, they crawled out at the shallow end and sat on the edge to catch their breath.

"Who won the last one?" Lonny asked, chest heaving.

"I don't rightly know," Ledyard replied, struggling to catch his own breath. "Let's settle it over a game of eight-ball."

"No fair, I don't have a pool table at home. With two here y'all probably got a lot more practice than I do."

"No," Ledyard shook his head. "I hardly ever play myself."

"Sure."

"Really. You'll probably beat me. I'm not that good."

"Okay," Lonny shrugged, "if you want."

Ledyard flashed his most devilish grin. "You done had it now, boy!"

"Oh come on!" Lonny protested.

"Just funnin' with ya," Ledyard laughed, hoisting himself off the side of the pool and standing up. "Come on."

Lonny jumped up and followed him to the pool table.

"Rack 'em up," Ledyard said, crossing to the cue stick holder mounted on the wall. "I'll get us a couple of sticks."

"Get me a good one," Lonny called as he squatted and fished the triangle from its holder in the table.

"They're all good ones," Ledyard answered, carefully selecting two sticks.

Looking across the tabletop, Lonny laughed, "I'll bet!"

He was setting the balls in the triangle when Ledyard returned with the cue sticks and handed him one. "Here, think this'll work?"

Lonny tested it on the table the way he'd seen his father do, rolling it back and forth. "Looks right good to me." He set the triangle, carefully lifted it off, picked up the stick and said, "Next time *you* rack and I break."

"Okay," Ledyard grinned, taking position behind the cue ball. He aimed and fired. There was a loud *crack!* as the wedge of balls scattered, the number seven dropping neatly into a corner pocket.

"You got solids," Lonny said.

"I know," Ledyard replied, moving around the table and into position once again. He took aim and fired the number four ball into a side pocket, moved around the table to meet the cue ball even before it stopped rolling and quickly fired the number one into a corner pocket. He paused, looking up at Lonny with a grin.

"That's pretty good, Led, but my dick's bigger," Lonny smirked.

"T'ain't, neither," Ledyard shot back.

"Oh yeah? C'mere."

Ledyard laid his cue stick on the table and went around to where Lonny was standing.

"Look," Lonny said, pulling his swimsuit down where it dropped around his ankles. "Can you do this?" Seemingly by magic his one-eyed friend slowly stood erect.

"Yeah, I can do that," Ledyard replied, letting his own swimsuit drop. As both boys looked on, he too, grew erect.

They both started laughing, Lonny admitting, "Say, that's pretty good, Led. I thought I was the only one who could do that!" Then he drew his forearm across the head, almost cringing with the sensation. "Wow! Ya ever rub it?"

"No," Ledyard replied, curiously drawing his arm across the way Lonny had, his knees almost buckling as he stammered, "W-Wow!"

The boys never heard Ledyard's parents' footsteps on the deep-pile carpet. But when they walked into the room anxious to meet their son's new friend, Brenda May's horrified shriek and her husband's angry exclamation had both boys diving to pull up their swimsuits in perfect unison like two puppets on strings.

"Oh my God!" Brenda May wailed, sinking to the floor, "My son's gay!"

Snarling like a pit bull, Pat Patterson crossed the room with angry strides, swatted his son a loud *thwack!* on the bottom and bellowed, "Get upstairs you little homo!"

Suddenly nauseous and trembling uncontrollably, Ledyard bolted from the room.

"And YOU!" Patterson roared, turning on the terrified Lonny. "Tryin' to turn my son queer! Where're your clothes?"

"In there, sir," Lonny managed to squeak, pointing towards the locker room.

"Well get in there and get dressed, you're a goin' home immediately!" Then the reverend strode over to his shaken wife and helped her up, embracing her soothingly. "There, there now, honey," he said, gently patting her shoulder. "Everything's goin' to be all right." After a moment he held her at arm's length. "Okay?"

She nodded numbly.

"Good. Now come over here and set while I phone for a car to get that boy out of here." He walked her over to one of the easy chairs by the fireplace, eased her into it, plopped into the matching chair, snatched a cordless phone off the end table and rapidly dialed the campus' front gate guardhouse.

"Hello? Sandy? Radio one of the patrol cars and have them scoot over to my house directly. Yes. There'll be a young'n waitin' out front. Have them drive the boy home. Yes, he'll be able to tell the driver where to go. Good."

He clicked the phone off, set it down and sat staring into space before his wife turned to him worriedly. "Oh, Pat, what're we goin' to do?"

"I been thinkin' about that," the reverend pondered, "and I think I'll just have this boy, what did Elly say his name was? Lonny? Yes, I'll just have this Lonny expelled from school."

Nervously twisting her hands in her lap, Brenda May said a quiet, "No."

Patterson turned on her with a frown. "No?"

"We can't do that, Pat, because we'll have to give them a reason. That boy's parents will have to have a reason, and, well, it could cause a big blowup, get in the papers and everything."

"Well, what then?"

"Tomorrow I'll go down and see the principal, Mr. Chambers, and simply explain to him that we feel this boy Lonny is a bad influence on our son and to see to it that they don't have any classes together."

"Hmmm. Yes, that might be best. And from now on we'll just make sure Ledyard always has a ride home from school. I don't think he's ready to handle anymore freedom for awhile."

"Yes, at least that way we'll make sure he doesn't have further contact with that, that *thing!*"

"I'm ready, reverend," Lonny barely breathed.

They both twisted around and stared at the little boy standing at the top of the steps leading from the pool area.

"You just wait right here, Brenda May," Patterson said, wearily heaving himself out of the chair and marching for the exit. "Let's go, young'n," he ordered, gesturing for Lonny to follow. Without a word Lonny trotted after him, down the hall, through the foyer and out the front door onto the massive, columned front porch.

"Sit down," Patterson indicated the steps.

Lonny did as he was told, drawing his knees up and wrapping his arms around them.

"Now I don't ever want to see you here again. You're not welcome. And furthermore, I'm a goin' to tell your teachers at school what happened, and if they catch you even *lookin'* at my son, let alone speakin' to him, I'm goin' to find out and YOU, young'n, are goin' to be in a peck of trouble. Do I make myself perfectly clear?"

"Yes, reverend," the boy whimpered, his hot face bright-red with shame.

"You should be ashamed of yourself."

"I am, sir," Lonny replied, choking back tears, "but please, *please* don't tell at school."

"Well..." Patterson wavered, then warned, "just don't talk to my son again *ever,* understand?"

"I won't, sir. Promise. Never."

"All right then, wait RIGHT here. A car's comin' to carry you home."

"Yes sir."

Without another word the reverend turned, stormed into the house and slammed the door.

Alone, trembling, ten-year-old Lonny Anderson, the toughest kid in the fifth grade, let the tears run hotly down his cheeks.

*   *   *

Quaking with fear and shame, Ledyard thought he was going to be sick and quickly shut his bathroom door and ran for the toilet. Standing over the bowl, though, the nauseousness faded. Vowing fervently to God that he would never again touch himself as long as he lived, he stepped into the shower still wearing his swimsuit. Turning the water on hot, he stood staring down at his feet, the water drumming steadily on his back until the relaxing warmth eased his trembling.

Calmed, he shut the water off, stepped out, snatched a towel off the rack and dried himself as he crossed to his dresser and pulled out a pair of red pajamas with racing cars all over them. Quickly slipping out of the wet swimsuit and tossing it to the bathroom tile, he jumped into the pajamas, returned to the bathroom, hung the suit up and went straight to bed and lay on his back with the covers pulled up to his chin.

He lay staring at the ceiling for a long time, endlessly repeating his vow to Jesus until the sheer monotony of the repetition weighed heavier and heavier on his eyelids.

He was fading, floating, on the verge of going under when it suddenly hit. A tingling sensation enveloped his entire body as a rapidly mounting pressure paralyzed him and the crescendo of a rushing sound grew to a roar in his ears. Terrified, he struggled to move, to escape, but found he couldn't even open his eyes, while at the same time there was a strange and frightening tugging, like something was trying to pull him apart from the inside out!

In a battle of wills with this huge, invisible thing pressing in from every side, Ledyard gathered all the strength of will power his mind could muster and through sheer mental determination managed to force his eyes open. In the snap of a finger it was gone.

He immediately sat up, wide-eyed, examining every inch of the room from his bed. And then it dawned on him. The "Invisible Ones." They had returned. But it certainly hadn't been like the last time when something had called him out to the walnut tree four years ago. That had been like a gentle urging. A coaxing. *This* had been scary, almost violent, like they were trying to pull his insides right out of his body!

Ledyard fell back on his pillow and stared at the ceiling with big, round eyes, almost afraid to breathe. What on earth was happening to him? Was this God's punishment sent straight from hell?

CLOUD DROPS

9

EARTHBOUND

> *[They are] raging waves of the sea, foaming out their own shame; wandering stars to whom is reserved the blackness of darkness forever.*
>
> *- JUDE 1:13*

It was time for another Earth mission, and with the rising of the sun came the rising of the children of God, assembly on the lawn and the launch.

Within moments they were streaking across the universe at the relatively *slow* speed of light. They wanted to do some sightseeing along the way. There was no hurry. Later they would simply accelerate to thought-speed and arrive within a thousandth of a second.

Upon entering the scope of Earth's solar system the team rapidly decelerated to light-speed. Streaking past Mars, they decelerated further, slowing to a hundred thousand miles per hour, a veritable crawl as they approached the blue globe of Earth and began scanning for Other Ones.

Other Ones, as the children of evil were referred to, generally stuck pretty close to Earth. Unable to attain thought-speed, or even the speed of light, and lacking guidance systems, these being gifts of God to *his* children, Other Ones were dreadfully afraid of interstellar space travel and rarely strayed even beyond the moon. Confined by the cold, dark vastness of space, they preferred the light and activity of Earth.

But their days were numbered and they knew it. Eventually God would visit upon them the "second death," when they would explode painlessly into atoms and become part of the universe. Stardust. For them, time and consciousness would cease to exist. Oblivion. Out of the blue and into the black. Period. The truth being that in their earthly incarnation they had overlooked the simple fact that one becomes exactly and precisely what one believes himself or herself to be. That when one says, "Oh, I think we all just become part of the universe when we die," *do* become part of the universe. Thus the creation of atoms, sub-atomic particles, and an ever-expanding universe. Likewise, those who believe they become the children of God, become God's children, thereby confirming Jesus' teaching that we are all self-actualizing creatures. Embittered with the realization that one doesn't *go* to hell, one *becomes* hell, Other Ones then amuse themselves by trying to lure Earthlings to a similar fate.

Even so, occasionally one would wander off into the vast wilderness with the insane idea that he could somehow find his way to heaven and con his way in—and would never be heard from again. As if the Kingdom of God were a place with gates and guards rather than a spiritual state of the soul. As if the Son of God had been joking when he said, "The Kingdom of God is within you."

Once, when Cambian and his team were returning from a mission, traversing the infinite darkness between the first and second galaxies, they spotted an Other One wobbling about, obviously lost and confused, darting this way and that and shrieking its anguished cries of fear, frustration, and loneliness.

Wondering what the heck it was doing way out there,

the team slowed and banked around in a tight circle for a closer look. Out of the scope of Earth's atmosphere they were forbidden to touch, but it was okay to look. It was the first time they'd seen one this far out.

As they slowly approached, the poor soul made a mad dash for the "ship," angrily demanding to be let aboard. The team easily and silently backed away at every headlong rush. Cursing and weeping, the creature screamed threats and repeatedly and furiously hurled beams of electrons at the "ship." This brought a burst of laughter from the team. It was like a peasant attacking a Russian T-34 tank with a stick.

One of the team, Andy, previously a history major crushed in an auto accident during spring break, said it looked and sounded like Adolf Hitler.

"Let's get out of here," Cambian said. The feeling was unanimous and with one thought they were gone.

Another time, in preparation for their responsibilities as members of a rescue squad on Earth duty back when the team was still in basic training, the Lord had taken them to a distant planet, the entire expanse of which was an incredible wasteland. A vast desert. Endless. Trackless.

After they landed and the Lord had quelled their idle chatter with a whispered command to *listen,* they heard a strange, eerie crying carried on the wind, vacillating from a high-pitched shriek of agony to a low, moaning groan of despair.

With his little group of trainees gathered closely around him, fear clearly etched on their youthful, innocent faces, Jesus asked solemnly, "What do you hear?"

"The desert crying out," Georgia, the cute little redhead answered.

"That's because the desert is a man, and each grain of sand is a part of his spirit, divided, broken, crying out to be whole again," Jesus softly intoned. "Ultimately, that is the nature of our mission on Earth—to bring together the spirit of man. That one becomes for all, and all becomes for one."

        *   *   *

Other Ones were frightened of everything. Even each other. Being an angry, bickering lot, they didn't hold hands in groups like the Elite, but rather, followed a policy of every man for himself. Thus they were hard to spot against the backdrop of stars. Even so, the team spotted three hurriedly scurrying around the dark side of the moon at the approach of the huge, light-pulsing disc, and then the gray team was slicing through the vapors and mists of Earth's upper stratosphere.

The "Captain" of the ship was always the one riding at the leading edge of the disc, but since everyone enjoyed playing Captain they took turns at it, changing Captains by simply rotating the disc. In addition, just for the fun of it they talked in "pilot language" while in flight, which they picked up from radio signals being transmitted between area aircraft and airport control towers. No one worried, though, that their own banter was accurate in any sense, but that, like children at play, it only *sounded* real.

At the moment, James was Captain, calling the signals as they streaked southward over Canada. "Air speed 50,000 miles per hour, altitude 80,000 feet and dropping," he said evenly.

Over Winnipeg, Manitoba, near the U.S. border, Debbie interrupted the chatter. "Got an auto accident spotted off the starboard side. Looks serious."

"Wonder where the red team is?" came the reply. Then, "Oh well, better do a go-round and have a look. Keep your eye on 'em, Deb."

"Will-Co Roger."

Ordinarily each team was assigned a specific district or nation in the world to cover and pretty much kept to their assigned areas, although if something serious were spotted and the other team unavailable, they would fill in for each other.

"Maintain altitude at 50,000, begin arc," James said in the same even voice as the ship banked into a tight curve. "What's it look like now, Deb?"

"Lot of blood. Looks like one'll be coming out."

"One of ours?"

"Just a moment—observing...."

Not *everyone* was rescued. The Elite could tell which were slated for recovery and which were not by the color of their auras. The unrescued, of course, was where Other Ones came from.

"Subject is out—definitely one of ours."

"Roger. Prepare to launch recovery squad."

"Negative, gray team, we've got it covered," André Lumière of the red "Maple Leaf" team interjected. From straight out of the east some 5,000 feet below, the red team came streaking to the scene.

"Abort recovery launch," James said, "and prepare to resume original flight plan."

As the ship arced around, James asked amicably, "Where've you lads been?"

"Had a busy morning in Montreal," came the reply.

"Yeah, you're looking a little light there."

"Three more to go and we're home."

"Well, good luck, gang."

"Take care."

The gray team resumed their original bearing as James relinquished the Captain's "chair" to Cambian, whose turn it was to take over. Within the boundaries of the patrol area the girls rarely played Captain. As the wingmen assigned to spotting trouble, as well as assessing a subject's aural status, they formed the recovery squads and had to be ready to drop out of the mother ship at a moment's notice to intercept the "newborns."

"How's everyone this morning?" Cambian asked, settling into his role as Captain.

There was a chorus of "A-Ok's," "Roger's," and "Ten-four's."

"Good, because after we've completed our rescue mission and the girls are on their way we've got another special assignment."

"With our young friend, Ledyard?" someone asked.

"You got it," Cambian answered evenly.

"Well we didn't have much luck last time," Andy put in.

"That's all right," Cambian assured him, "if we keep at it we'll succeed—I hope."

"And then what?" James asked.

"And then we scatter like jackrabbits. And the next thing, he'll be all alone, scared witless, and return home so fast we'll have to be careful we don't get sucked in by the vacuum!"

At that everyone laughed.

As they passed over Duluth, Minnesota at 50,000 feet, Cambian asked, "Anybody see anything?"

"Looks pretty quiet in Duluth today," Natalie answered.

Over Minneapolis they spotted a three-car accident with two fatalities, but neither of the subjects was one of "theirs" and they kept their course heading as the two newly generated Other Ones, a Baptist minister from Indianapolis and a Protestant lawyer from Cincinnati, hurled past crying in terror of the unknown.

Over the Western Suburbs of Chicago things started getting a little more interesting. Michelle spotted a kid in a car parked in a forest preserve who had just shot-up cocaine and accidentally overdosed.

"Yep, he's one of ours," she said evenly.

"Prepare to launch recovery squad," Cambian intoned.

"Ready to launch," Debbie, Natalie, and Michelle said

in unison.

"Go for it!"

The three girls, the fiery auras of their travel-wheels waxing white-hot, dropped from the mother ship in a tri-part formation. Streaking to intercept the terrified youth tumbling out of control as the Earth, in a reversal of gravity, spit him heavenward, Debbie called out, "I've got this one!"

Natalie and Michelle veered off to either side as Debbie made a perfect interception. Like a line-drive smack into a third baseman's mitt, she had him.

Now, hiding out in a cloud, or in the absence of clouds, drifting along on the upper jet stream well above commercial air traffic lanes, she would assist her young charge in adjusting to the reality of his present condition. Maybe give him a few flying lessons. Meanwhile, Natalie and Michelle would scout for other subjects to rescue, perhaps return to the ship, the whole squad continuing on to make further recoveries as they went. Once Natalie and Michelle had their own "newborns" they would regroup with Debbie and return to Universe Center as a unit.

Cambian could tell they were in for a rough day. Even before Michelle and Natalie rejoined the ship, he spotted a tragedy in the making. He said nothing. They were forbidden to touch suicide cases, and none of the team members would even want to know about it, let alone watch.

Awaiting the unfortunate soul was a box with invisible walls wherein he would be contained and cast into the deepest, darkest regions of space. There he would remain, alone, conscious, with all his thoughts and memories, to circle endlessly in his little prison cell unto the day of judgment.

And how long until judgment day? No one knew. But if it was only a hundred years, that would be a long time in solitary confinement. The teenaged boy, not yet 17, despondent over some sweetheart romance gone sour, started his car and closed the garage door. Cambian looked away.

Then all hell broke loose. A five-car pileup on the Eisenhower expressway near Chicago had three dead, one coming their way. Just as Georgia dropped from the ship to join Natalie and Michelle for the recovery, James spotted a man in an alley holding another at bay with a pistol.

James zeroed in on the gunman and took a telepathic reading. "Look," he said to Cambian, pointing.

"Got a reading?"

"Yep, sounds like he's gonna shoot, too."

They never attempted to intervene without first taking a telepathic reading of the assailant, verifying his intention to do physical violence. Thus they avoided startling a perpetrator into an attack that was not originally planned.

"Andy, James, you game?"

They were.

"Okay, let's see what we can do."

Avery took command of the ship as Andy, James, and Cambian dropped away and streaked to the scene below.

There wasn't really a lot they could do, of course. Forbidden from even showing themselves, their powers were extremely limited. Furthermore, intervening in Earthly events was not their primary purpose. Nevertheless, on more than one occasion they had managed to save the victim of a violent crime by reducing to their lowest ebb (thus maintaining invisibility) and suddenly dropping into the midst of the situation and causing an increase in pressure-per-square-inch that slowed or otherwise distracted the assailant at a critical moment, allowing the victim to escape or repel the attack.

Another tactic they often used was to form a triangle with a separation of five feet between corners, settle around the assailant right at ear level, and then talk to one another telepathically. (Actually, all of their communications were telepathic.) If the assailant were sober, or even if he weren't, he might pick up on it with his own dormant telepathic powers and think he was *hearing* voices. The criminal thus startled, again the victim might escape or otherwise repel the attack.

The team arrived in less than five seconds, hovering ten feet overhead, assessing the situation and waiting for just the right moment to make their move.

"You owe me, Barry," the gunman was saying.

"I know, I know," Barry blurted nervously. "Just gimme a week. One week. Friday I'll have it, I swear!"

"That's what you said last week and the week before, and the week before that and every time I seen you for the last year." The gunman paused, his voice taking on a deadly tone. "You're makin' a fool outta me, Barry. People are startin' to talk. Startin' to think maybe I'm goin' soft, and I just can't allow that to happen. I got too much paper floatin', know what I mean? So I gotta make an example, Barry. Today it's you."

"Please! Please!"

"Say goodbye, Barry." Just as he extended the gun, aiming it pointblank between Barry's eyes, he was startled by what he thought was the voice of someone standing directly behind him. His stomach dropping out with sudden fear, he turned, muttering a confused, "Huh?"

Barry had nothing to lose and leapt. As the two men tumbled to the gritty concrete, the gun went off in Barry's gut with a muffled *bang!* as meat, blood, and whitish-gray backbone chips blew into the air.

In a reflex of disgust the invisble observers shut their eyes. When they looked again, Cambian was calling for Natalie and Michelle.

"Roger," the girls answered in unison, "we'll *both* get this one." And then Barry found himself warm in their arms.

CLOUD DROPS

10

THE LARGER WHEEL OF LIFE

> *Be not overcome of evil, but overcome evil with good.*
> *- ROMANS 12:21*
>
> *And there appeared [above] them, cloven tongues like as fire....*
> *- ACTS 2:3*

It had been a rough day, but the girls were on their way home now, their precious cargos safe and warm inside them. Normally the guys would have been heading back to Universe Center too, but not this time. They still had another job to do. At the moment, though, they were kicking back on a cloud drifting somewhere over west Texas.

Contemplating the next phase of their mission, the discussion turned to James' going away party—and just where he was going. He had been with the team for over five years now and had decided to take on a new adventure.

All the team members in all the rescue squads were volunteers and could put in for reassignment at any time. There was an infinite variety of duties, tasks, or simply enjoyable activities that one could elect to take on, just as there was an infinite variety of planets, with an infinite variety of cultures and civilizations at various stages of development, from the most primitive to the most sophisticated, all of which needed key figures to appear at important moments to spur along a fledgling society, or to help avert disaster at critical points in the more sophisticated ones. (Such as Einstein appearing on the American scene at the approach of World War Two and spurring along the development of the atomic bomb, a technological advance that would have been disastrous had the Nazis, let alone some of America's allies of the time, claimed it first.)

The universe itself being infinite, there was room for an infinitely expanding population, which was the ultimate goal of God. To populate the universe. Nevertheless, transforming biological life forms, humans, into super-humans, came with the inherent risk of spreading super-human evil throughout the universe. (Not unlike a spreading cancer devouring a human body.) Thus was it necessary that Earth, and the process of life itself, become a sort of giant threshing machine separating the wheat from the chaff, the good from the evil.

Evil then, spawned of Satan in his bitter desire to consume mankind, became merely a cog in the larger wheel of life. A mechanism. An instrument of God's. Thus would Other Ones be contained in the vicinity of Earth unto the day of judgment, regardless of whether mankind would finally vanquish evil, ushering in an era of peace, prosperity, and goodwill for all mankind, or whether cataclysmic violence would engulf the world, with the consequent nuclear war and utter collapse of civilization.

And although God was ready and willing to help Earthlings by any means, his powers were limited by his own desire for, on the one hand, creating life, and on the other, containing evil. For God to simply step in and undo the evil *now* would be to undo the process whereby newly generated humans could aspire to the more abundant life of the Elite.

Furthermore, although evil might exist all around the world, as in the Other Ones, it could not exist *in* the world if mankind refused to give it hands. Thus could mankind contain evil (by refusing it), or they could allow it to run rampant (by taking part in it). But evil, falling within the realm of the spiritual, would never be defeated through political or legalistic means because one cannot legislate that which resides in the hearts of men and women.

That mankind might somehow outrun the evil on Earth by constructing mechanisms of space flight and escaping to other planets would be, as deliberately designed by God, impossible. Bound by the elementary laws of physics, the distances were just too great.

So Earthlings were at a critical moment in their development, torn between the wonders of their recent technological advances, with the belief that this might somehow save them, and the simple truth that only their own spiritual awakening could provide the answer.

In short, technology, although important and capable of much, would be useless as a tool for achieving universal peace and prosperity in a world filled with spiritually dead human beings, because the technology simply would not be appropriately applied. (As when societies build tanks instead of tractors, or when governments in a world filled with starving millions pay farmers *not* to grow food.)

But this wasn't what the boys were discussing as they drifted along on their cloud. They were discussing James' future, or about to, when Avery interrupted with, "Hey, where're we at?"

Cambian crawled to the cloud's edge and stuck his head out. "Oh, somewhere east of San Antonio and catching a nice Westerly. Should get to Houston right on time." He returned to where the others were comfortably sprawled and settled back on his pillow, one foot up on the other.

"So, James, you were going to tell us about your plans," Andy said as soon as everyone was settled.

"Yes, I'm really looking forward to it," James replied. "There's this planet in the 487th galaxy of the third quadrant of the fifth universe that's quite advanced. With an international forum founded on democratic principles overseeing international relations, and food, clothing, housing and education available for the entire population of the planet, there hasn't been even a small civil war in over 30 years. And it's looking really good that things will only get better.

"Anyway, they've already started building their first undersea city, which will be devoted to mining and undersea farming, and I'm going to be born there and become a marine biologist. I already picked out my parents on the SuperViewer at the library when we were back home last week, and I'm really excited about it. In fact I can hardly wait!"

"How does that work, about picking out your parents and stuff?" Avery asked curiously. "I haven't even looked into any of this yet."

"Me either," Andy said.

"I don't think any of us have yet," Cambian put in.

"Well, depending on what it is you want to do or why you've chosen a place, or in some cases if you've volunteered for a special assignment, you can either pick your parents or go for random selection. I picked mine because I knew exactly what I wanted to do and where I wanted to be born—in this underwater city."

"Yeah, so then what?" Andy asked, sitting up.

"Well, when the time comes they put you to sleep and like, freeze-condense your entire body (aural-electrical field) into a seed-pod so tiny it can't be seen by the naked eye." James paused, looking around at his teammates. "You followin' so far?"

Everyone nodded, Cambian saying, "I think so."

"Okay, so you're in this little seed-pod, sound asleep, and put into this launcher that's primed for thought-speed and triggered by the targeted host-parents at the exact moment of conception. Then, through electrostatic induction you're fired in. Priority rating, you know," James grinned. "As far as appearance goes," he hastened to add, "it'll simply be my electrical taking on their biological. I'll inherit their genes—I'll look like them."

"Yeah, well you can't tell everything from the Super-Viewer, my man," Avery piped up. "What if later they decide to abort for some reason?"

"Or break up a month after you've been launched?" Andy put in.

"Or turn out to be a couple of drunks that end up livin' in a culvert under a highway?" Avery sang out in rhythm.

"Hold on, lads, I can only answer one question at a time!" James laughed. "Okay, if they abort it's called a misfire and I return to Universe Center and the library and the process of selection starts all over.

"If they happen to break up after I'm launched there's no telling where I could end up. That's the chance you take. That's what makes it an adventure. And besides, as you know, in the overall scheme of things it's a pretty short life in the skin. I'll be back here sittin' on a cloud with you guys before ya know it!" he concluded with a grin.

"You won't be able to bring your girls," Andy pointed out.

"That's all right. I'm sure I'll meet a nice girl down there when I'm of age. And I'm sure you guys won't mind looking after my women until I get back, if they even elect to hang around waiting, which I doubt."

"Aye-aye on that!" Avery laughed. "You'll catch up with them somewhere over the rainbow!"

There was a lapse of silence broken by Cambian. "Well, it sounds like a lot of fun, but all that getting reborn stuff's not for me."

"What you going to do, Cambian?" Avery asked.

Cambian pondered. "Well, at the moment I've got to finish up the present project, which is going to take awhile. But when that's done," he shrugged, "I'm not sure. I've heard of planets that have a certain classification, like if they don't have humans yet, or if the human life forms are still primitive enough and you don't materialize right in front of them, you can go there and explore. You know, come and go at will without the necessity of being born."

"Yeah, I heard a that," Avery said.

"Right," Cambian continued, "and there's this one planet that has trees as tall as America's tallest skyscrapers with trunks as big around, mountains that rise tens of miles with valleys just as deep. And primitive cultures. Little tribes, really. The cool thing is that they make their homes in these massive tree trunks, hollowing out little rooms with windows around the outer edges, the trees becoming like high-rise apartment buildings. But they avoid the core so it doesn't kill the trees. Anyway, I was thinking if I can get clearance I might go there, do a little exploring or what not, and maybe introduce the God concept."

"Hey, that's a great idea, my man!" Avery exclaimed. "If I can get my ladies interested, could we come too?"

"Sure," Cambian answered easily, "the more the merrier, I always say!"

"What about you, Andy?" James asked, turning to him.

"I'm not sure yet," Andy shrugged. "I've always been interested in medieval times. Knights, castles, stuff like that. There's more than one planet at that stage. I might just go for the reborn thing like you, James, with an eye towards inventing the telescope or something."

"Oh, the Galileo type gig, huh?" Avery piped up.

Again Andy shrugged, "Yeah, maybe."

James let out a long, low whistle. "You sure, mate? I mean, look what they did to Galileo for pointing out that the Earth revolved around the sun."

"Yeah, but maybe there won't be any Catholics where I'm going," Andy chuckled. "And like you said, James, it's a short trip in the skin, and under medieval conditions I'm sure it'll be even shorter. And I think it would be the greatest to, you know, actually *be* there, in those times, on a planet more or less like Earth. It'll be like time traveling!"

"Which brings to mind the memory factor," Avery suddenly spoke up. "I mean, if you dudes are goin' to be put to sleep and the next thing you know you a squallin' baby again takin' his first breath, well, how much of your present life *here* are you goin' to remember, if at all? And at what age do you start rememberin'?"

"Good question," James answered, "and one I've looked into." He paused, frowning with thought, then continued. "The way I understand it there *is* a memory loss. Almost total, actually. But then as you grow older, different things, a sound, a smell, the way the sunlight angles through a window one afternoon, might spark a memory. A sort of déjà vu. Of course as you grow older and these experiences start piling up, I suppose you come to some kind of realization in a vague sort of way."

"Sounds eerie to me, man," Avery said.

"Sounds interesting to me," Andy countered.

"And it sounds like it's time to see where we're at," Cambian interjected. "Could be time for a cloud-drop." Getting to his hands and knees, he crawled to the edge for a look and then returned to the group. "We're just outside of Houston now. Another minute or so and we'll be right over the target area, so let's go over the plan."

Everyone sat up and gathered close around Cambian. "Okay," he began, "Avery's going to provide paralysis and electric to keep vital organs functioning in case the boy comes out, right?"

"You got it, my man," Avery replied.

"You remember the procedure we followed last time?"

Avery nodded, reciting, "Foot-to-foot, hand-to-hand, forehead-to-forehead."

"Right. Then James, Andy and I will set up the tri-part trajectory beam. But be careful you don't get so involved you generate too much energy and ignite the atmosphere. Lot of nitrogen and oxygen in this stuff, don't forget, and we don't want to scare the kid to death or set him on fire. As you know we can't *force* him to come out, all we can do is coax, encourage, and provide the conduit of escape, but it does take a willful decision on his part."

"And if we get him out?" Andy asked.

"The moment you feel separation, scatter. He'll be moving so fast and be so distracted he'll never even know we were there." He turned to Avery, "Then you just maintain your station. The moment the boy returns, and it won't take long, you evaporate."

"Right." Avery gave a single nod of assent.

Cambian turned to the group at large. "Any questions?"

Everyone shook their heads, Andy commenting, "No, I think everyone's got it."

"Good. Let's go downstairs and prepare to drop."

"Downstairs" was merely the bottom of the cloud from which they could watch the Earth below and drop out at the right moment.

"There's the campus," Avery said as the four of them lay down on their stomachs and poked their heads out for a look.

"And the house," James put in.

"Got a fix on it?" Cambian asked.

"Right-O. The lad's just getting into bed now."

"All right, guys," Cambian said as they all joined hands in preparation for the drop, "get ready, 'cause we want to catch him *before* he goes to sleep. Otherwise, he'll just think it's a dream and we'll never get him out."

As the flaming-red sun sank beneath the rolling green hills of southeastern Texas, the boys, like parachutists holding hands in a circle, dropped from the cloud and plummeted to Earth some 10,000 feet below.

"Don't forget," Cambian shouted above the roar of the wind, "once we're inside, *whisper.*"

All their communications being telepathic, a "whisper" was simply an extremely low-level transmission. An effort on the team's part to reduce as much as possible the mental-electrical interference the targeted subject would have to endure during the operation. (Which Ledyard would experience as a roaring in his ears.)

At 1,000 feet they rapidly decelerated and silently passed through the roof, the attic, and the maid's quarters. Once inside Ledyard's room they hovered near the ceiling for a momentary assessment of the situation, then went to work.

Avery moved first, gently settling over the boy, who lay upon his back, enveloping him from head to foot and electrically paralyzing him. There was an immediate reaction as revealed in the rapid movement of the youth's eyes beneath his lids, which began fluttering as he struggled to open them and found that he could not.

Immediately Cambian, Andy and James moved in, one at each shoulder, with Cambian hovering just above Ledyard's midsection. The head would lead the rest of the boy's body (aural-electrical field).

"Careful, now," Cambian muttered as they gradually increased power and tried to literally suck the boy's aural-electrical field out of the meat of his body and launch it through the conduit they had set up.

The "conduit," an invisible electron beam pouring off Cambian's back, shot straight through the ceiling where it pierced the rest of the house and disappeared into the sky.

"He's fighting hard, I don't know how long I can hold him!" Avery whispered harshly, grunting with the exertion of his efforts.

"Okay, boys," Cambian said evenly, "let's increase power just a little bit."

Cambian felt the surge of increased flow. It was starting to grow warm at his back where the beam exited. Further increase and they were risking an ignition, which would appear as nips of blue flame in midair directly over Ledyard. They were just about maxed-out and Cambian knew it.

"Boy, this kid has a strong field!" Avery exclaimed.

"Hold him, hold him," Cambian quietly rallied his team. "Another 30 seconds and maybe he'll let go."

Avery's struggle was beginning to become apparent. "I don't think I can hold him that long, he's really starting to come on strong!"

Cambian considered increasing power a notch more, but decided it wasn't worth risking a flameout. This was going to be tougher than he thought. "Okay," he said in the same even-tempered whisper, "prepare to evacuate." He paused while everyone got ready for a uniform withdrawal, then issued the command, "Evacuate!"

Instantly they withdrew as one. Sucked up the beam of their own creation, they passed silently through the ceiling for the heavens and the universe beyond.

CLOUD DROPS

11

BACK AT THE RANCH

> *...Jesus answereth again, and saith unto them, Children, how hard it is for them that trust in riches to enter into the kingdom of God!*
>
> *- MARK 10:24*

Fourteen-year-old Ledyard Patterson jerked upright in bed, wide-eyed, scanning the darkness, heart pounding. His breathing gradually returned to normal, the panic receding as he realized he'd only been dreaming about his last experience two years ago when whatever it was had invisibly paralyzed him and tried to... *pull him out of his body* was the only way he could think to describe it.

Throwing the blanket aside, he got out of bed in the chilly darkness and went to the bathroom. Returning, he suddenly paused, glanced up at the ceiling, and quietly said, "Y'all are right, I'd better jot that down."

He went to his desk and in the moonlight scribbled a quick note on a legal pad next to his computer; *Who's to say Jesus isn't in heaven right now, saying to Mohammed, "Any friend of yours is a friend of mine?"*

Frowning, Ledyard took a step back and looked up at the ceiling again. "Meanin' what?" he questioned, then cocked his head as if listening.

87

"Oh, right." He returned to his desk and jotted; *Reference St. John 14:6... Jesus saith unto him, I am the way, the truth, and the life: no man cometh unto the Father but by me.*

Ledyard examined what he had written for a thoughtful moment, laid the pen down and started for his bed when it occurred to him what was happening. He froze in his tracks and looked up at the ceiling again. The "Invisible Ones" were back! Talking to him in their strange, voiceless way. Feeding him little tidbits of information the way they always did.

Then he was struck by a thought. Maybe the Invisible Ones who spoke to him by the walnut tree when he was six, and who just spoke to him now, as they occasionally had down through the years, were one and the same with the force that tried twice in the past to pull him out of his body!

Even from the first they had always spoken to him through some sort of mental process that he supposed must be telepathy. But telepathy didn't exist. Or so he'd been taught. Well maybe at school they were wrong.

He returned to bed and pulled the blankets up. Frowning with concentration, he struggled to communicate like them. To mentally send a message to whoever was out there. To tell them to come back and talk to him. To ask if they were the ones who tried pulling him out of his body. Then it occurred to him, *it was just like praying.*

*   *   *

Ledyard woke up before his alarm clock went off. Remembering to disengage it, he got out of bed, went to the bathroom and took a shower. Unable to shower away the thoughts plaguing him, he turned to them instead.

He was ten the first time they tried pulling him out. The second time was two years later when he was 12. If this was some sort of consistent pattern they followed then it would be happening again. Soon. And Ledyard *knew* he could go with them, whoever they were, if he'd just lay back and relax instead of always fighting it like he did. But how did he know it wasn't the devil who would then cart him straight off to hell? How did he know he wouldn't die?

Another disturbing aspect: although they didn't seem to have any trouble responding to questions pertaining to whatever they were trying to tell him, later when the "session" was over and he had composed a few of his own questions, they were always gone. If they were really some benevolent, supernatural force or God or whatever, weren't they always, in a sense, present?

Ledyard stepped out of the shower, toweled-off, dressed for school and was about to go down to breakfast when he noticed the note he had scribbled during the night. He picked it up. Boy, he thought, reading through it, his daddy wasn't going to be happy with this idea, either.

In the kitchen, Elly was at the counter making his parent's usual breakfast of, lately, some concoction of health cereal. His parents hadn't come down yet and he put his books on the table and slipped into a chair at his usual place.

Glancing over her shoulder, Elly said, "Mornin', Led."

"Mornin', Elly."

"Gettin' started early, eh?"

Ledyard shrugged. "Just woke up early for some reason."

"What you be havin' dis mornin'?"

"Oh, let's see... how about bacon and eggs?"

"You got it, child." There was a clatter as she dug out the fry pan and set it on the stove, then turned to the refrigerator and got the bacon out.

Hearing the bacon sizzle as it hit the pan, Ledyard looked up to see his parents come in.

"Coffee, Elly," the reverend said rather coarsely as they took their places at the table.

"Right away, sir."

"Mornin', Ledyard."

"Daddy, mamma," Ledyard said.

Both his parents could tell something was bothering their son but pretended not to notice. Lately they'd had some awfully heated discussions with plenty of red-faced yelling on both sides, and they didn't want to get into another one of *those*.

Turning to his wife, the reverend said, "I talked to Harry Wigglesworth after the show last night and he said receipts were up higher than ever. Said the recent revisions on my seed-faith approach were really startin' to pay off."

"That's wonderful, dear," Brenda May said with a sunny smile. "See, I told you that one would be a winner."

"And," the reverend continued cheerfully, "he says t'ain't no end in sight. That it'll work for as long as I want to keep it goin'."

"Well we can sure use the money," Brenda May intoned as Elly set cups of coffee before both of them.

The reverend laughed, brushing aside a lock of light-brown hair that had fallen across his forehead. "Hell, we're goin' to be pullin' in so much green we'll have to increase Granger's trips..." his voice suddenly fell off. With an uncomfortable glance at Ledyard, he cleared his throat and started again. "Uh, what I meant to say was, uh, that...."

"That Granger would be able to take more vacations," his wife quickly interjected with a bright smile.

"Yes, that's what I meant to say."

Elly brought breakfast on a huge tray, set the various orders before them and paused, asking, "Everything okay dis mornin', sir?"

"Fine, fine," the reverend replied a little more sharply than he intended, irritated at himself for his lapse of common sense in front of Ledyard, as well as the maid, and then having to have his wife bail him out.

"Daddy?" Ledyard hesitantly queried after Elly had left.

"What?"

"How do we know there's no such thing as telepathy?"

The reverend turned on him sharply, but caught himself before speaking and heaved a sigh instead. Composing himself, he answered evenly, "Because it's not in the Bible."

"But jet planes aren't in the Bible and *they* exist."

The reverend slammed a hand to the table, "Now look, boy, don't start with me this mornin'!"

Taken aback at the ferocity of the outburst, Ledyard said, "Fine," and got up and left the table, grabbing his books as he went and ignoring the angry demands of his father to come back.

Granger was just pulling up the drive when the angry teenager stormed out of the house and slammed the door behind him.

"You can't allow him to get you so upset like that, darlin'," Brenda May said, laying a soothing hand on her husband's arm.

He roughly yanked his arm away. "I think that young'n is losin' his mind," he frowned. "I mean, here I've sweated and struggled to build this empire, and it's as if instead of wantin' to step into my shoes he wants to destroy them!" He sighed, shaking his head. "I just don't get it!"

"He's at that rebellious age, Pat. You know how 14-year-old boys are."

"No." Momentarily lost in thought, the reverend shook his head. "No, his mind is startin' to go. I really believe it's the beginnin' of God's punishment for his homosexual tendencies. Apparently he has not, in his heart of hearts, fully repented of his sexual sin."

*   *   *

"Don't pick me up until 6:00 o'clock," Ledyard said to Granger as he got out of the limousine in front of school. "I've got football practice this afternoon."

"Very good, sir," Granger said, firmly shutting the car door.

Eighth grade had come as a great relief for Ledyard. It had been a real battle, but he'd finally managed to get his parents to let him join the football team after pointing out how small some of the other players were. Quickly distinguishing himself as an excellent receiver, after a lifetime of social isolation he had at last formed some real friendships. And he had it all planned out, too. Football in the fall, basketball in the winter, baseball in the summer.

Granger stood by the long, black limousine watching until Ledyard was inside the building, just as he'd done for the last eight years of the boy's school career, then got in the car and left.

That was the other nice thing about being in junior high. Now the students weren't required to wait outside until the bell rang for classes to begin, but could go to the cafeteria to study, which spared Ledyard the stigma of being forced to go inside ahead of everyone else. And although many of his classmates were still somewhat distant and uncomprehending as to why he always came and went in a chauffeured limousine, as part of the football team no one dared ridicule him—at least no one not on the team.

When Ledyard walked into the cafeteria, a group of his teammates waved to him from a table at the far end where they always sat. Ledyard joined them, tossing his books on the table and sitting down.

"That was a great reception last Friday, Led," Roger, the team's quarterback and Ledyard's best friend, said for the umpteenth time since the play last weekend. And this was only Monday.

"Ah," Ledyard waved him off, "I just got lucky."

"Heck, you always say that." Roger lived on campus with his widowed mother, a ministry secretary. A bit on the chunky side with a round face and rather large, crewcut head, he could really fire off a pass.

At the same table, two chairs removed, Jeff, Doug, and Tom were huddled together snickering conspiratorially while casting secret glances Ledyard's way.

Roger noticed. "Y'all got a problem?" he asked with a dark frown.

"Nothin' 'bout you, buffalo breath," Jeff sneered, while his two co-conspirators grinned and waved.

"Hey Ledyard," Jeff called.

Ledyard turned. "What?"

"Will you do me a favor?"

"What?"

"The next time God speaks to your daddy's heart will you get it on tape for me?" The three boys broke up, laughing hysterically and pounding the table.

Ledyard turned back to Roger, who was glowering at them. "Forget it, bud."

"I don't like 'em talkin' 'bout the reverend that way even if he weren't your daddy," Roger said coldly.

Ledyard just stared at him, heaved a sigh, sat back in his chair and folded his hands behind his head. "I really need to talk to you, Roger."

Roger turned back to Ledyard. "'Bout what?"

"No. I want to talk to you alone."

"Take a walk?" Roger offered.

Ledyard nodded, gathering up his books. "Yeah."

"Hey, where y'all goin'?" Jeff asked as Ledyard and Roger pushed their chairs back and got up to leave.

"No place, buffalo breath," Roger said, leaning in Jeff's face before they walked off.

With ten minutes until the first bell, they took a back-door out and walked through a grove of trees behind the school.

Ledyard paused, taking a deep breath. "Roger," he began, "there's somethin' I never told you—or anyone else, either."

Roger nodded. "You look like you got somethin' real serious a weighin' on your mind."

Ledyard hesitated, then asked in a low voice as if someone might be hiding nearby listening, "Do you believe in God?"

Roger looked at his friend curiously. "What kind of question is that? You know I do."

"I mean really *really* believe in him?"

After a thoughtful moment Roger slowly nodded. "Well, uh, t'ain't really sure what you mean by that, but I believe in God, cross my heart and hope to die if I'm lyin'." He stopped walking and turned to his friend. "And do you want to know why, Ledyard?"

"Why?"

"Because when I was six years old my dog got hit by a car. Now my mamma told me this," he cautioned, "so you can believe it. She said the vet come, looked at Sparky, and told her to let him take it. That my dog wouldn't make it till mornin'."

Roger shook his head. "Nope, mamma wouldn't let him take Sparky. And she said all that night I stayed on my knees in the livin' room just a prayin' over and over again askin' God not to let Sparky die. Sure enough, next mornin' a beam a sunlight come a shinin' through the kitchen window and fell on Sparky's head where he was all curled up on a blanket by the stove."

Chuckling at the memory, Roger continued, "My mamma said that dog's head come up just like he was hearin' the voice a God, an' then ol' Sparky got right up an' trotted into the livin' room where I was still on my knees prayin' and licked my face. And it, like, took me outta this prayin' trance I was in and after that, well, I *still* got Sparky to this day!"

Ledyard swallowed. "That's some story, Roger."

"And every word of it true."

"I believe you," Ledyard said. He paused, then asked uneasily, "Would you believe me if I said that since I was six years old I think God, or maybe angels, have been talkin' to me?"

For a long moment Roger didn't say anything. Then he turned to Ledyard with a funny look on his face and said, "Sort'a runs in the family, huh?"

"Heck, I don't rightly know, Roger," Ledyard said in dead earnest.

"What'd they sound like?"

"Wait. Do you believe me?"

"I c'ain't say, Ledyard. That sounds pretty strange. What'd they sound like?"

"Wait. Y'all believe it when my daddy says on television that God speaks to him, don't ya?"

Roger hesitated. "Well, yeah," he finally admitted.

"Well I don't," Ledyard immediately replied.

"What!?" Roger exclaimed in astonishment.

"That's right, Roger. These angels, or whatever they are, keep tellin' me things totally contrary to what my daddy says God has told *him!*"

Gaping in disbelief, Roger's voice rose, "Like what, I'd be right pleased to know?"

"Like, they told me last night that Mohammed, you know, the Moslem prophet, that he's in heaven right now and that Jesus is a friend of his!"

"So?"

"So don't you see?" Ledyard cried emphatically. "That means, as a rule, Moslems don't go to hell as my daddy—no—as all Christianity teaches. And therefore we shouldn't be fightin' them. Sure, it's a different religion, but under the same God!"

Roger remained silent for several moments. "But how do you know it ain't the devil just tryin' to confuse and trick you?" he finally asked. "Ya know, like, tryin' to get you against your daddy because his ministry is doin' so well?"

"That's just what I want you to help me figure out, Roger."

"Well what in the blue sky of heaven do they sound like?"

Ledyard shook his head. "They don't make any sound, Roger. They talk to me telepathically."

"T'ain't no such thing as telepathy."

"So my daddy says!"

Taken aback at Ledyard's indignation, Roger said, "Wow, I never realized you were havin' such differences with your daddy."

"Roger," Ledyard intoned, "there's somethin' else. About every two years, twice now, once when I was ten and once when I was 12, they tried pullin' me out of my body. At least I *think* it was them."

"Pull you out of your body?" Roger stared at him.

"Yeah. I... I really don't know how to describe it except to say it sure felt like that to me."

"What stopped them?"

"Me, Roger. I stopped them. That's the weird thing. It's like they're tryin' to coax me out, but if I don't want to go t'ain't a thing they can do about it. The only question worryin' me is, if I go with them will I die? Are they demons that'll cart me straight off to hell?"

"Heck, I don't know about that, Led," Roger said, shaking his head. "You sure ya haven't been studyin' too hard lately or somethin'?"

"Hang it all, you don't believe me!" Ledyard exclaimed accusingly.

Roger stopped and turned to face his friend. "No, I didn't say that. It's just that, well, I don't know *what* you're askin' me to believe. It don't make sense to me."

Ledyard calmed down. "Okay. I can understand that. But just tell me one thing. This bunch, whoever they are, seem to work in a pattern. Accordin' to my past experience they should be showin' up anytime now for another pull-and-tug session. What I'm ponderin' is, should I go with them?"

Roger thought about it for some time as they turned and started back for the school. At last he asked solemnly, "Are ya feelin' right with God?"

"As right as I'll ever feel."

"All right, then," Roger shrugged, "you don't got a thing to lose. God will be watchin' after your immortal soul. If they come back, go along, callin' on the name of the Lord. I don't care if it's Satan himself ridin' the seven-headed dragon, as long as you're callin' on Jesus you'll be safe." He paused. "Do you believe that?"

Ledyard stared at him, then nodded. "Yes," he said quietly, "yes I do."

CLOUD DROPS

12

THE PROPHET AND THE PREACHER

> *And he put forth the form of an hand, and*
> *took me by a lock of mine head; and the*
> *spirit lifted me up between the earth and the*
> *heaven.*
>
> *- EZEKIEL 8:3*

After dinner, with an hour or so to kill before the rally his father was staging to burn rock albums, Ledyard kicked back on the couch in the recreation room to watch TV. As the big screen came to life, a preacher that reminded Ledyard of Jimmy Swaggart was strutting about the screen, red-faced, fierce-eyed and shouting, "These liberal-minded, weak-kneed bleedin' heart humanists are takin' over the country, corrupting our youth, and plantin' the seeds of atheism through *television!*" He dabbed at his brow with a hanky. "And it doesn't stop there! You've got the Buddhists! The Nudists! The Hinduists! The Shirley McClainists! Channelers, flim-flammers and I don't know what all!"

Ledyard was looking forward to the rally. Not the burning of rock albums necessarily, which he thought was stupid, but for the opportunity to get out and do a little socializing on a Friday night. They were going to have a big bonfire and a lot of girls from school would be there. In the week since talking to Roger, his "Invisible Friends" had not returned.

He looked up at the TV and switched channels. Dwight Thompson strode onto the screen as his father strode into the room. "Can I talk with you a moment, son?"

"Sure, daddy," Ledyard said, reaching for the control unit and lowering the volume.

The reverend hitched up his pants, sat down next to his son and started right in. "I didn't mean to be so sharp with you the other mornin', it's just that lately you've been sayin' some mighty disturbin' things." He paused, clearing his throat. "What I want to know is, where've you been gettin' these weird ideas from?"

Ledyard shifted uncomfortably. "Well, that's what I wanted to talk about before, daddy."

"I know, telepathy," his father interjected in a rare, perceptive moment. "Son, what you're tellin' me is that you're hearin' voices."

"No!" Ledyard exclaimed, "I'm *not* hearin' voices. I'm like," he shrugged, "I don't know, receivin' messages that seem to be comin' directly to my mind from... from outer space or somethin'!"

The reverend nodded understandingly. "I know, son, but that's just not within the bounds of what we call reality. Do you understand?"

Ledyard adamantly shook his head. "No. It's not just these messages. I've actually felt a... a *presence* in the room with me. The first time was when I was six and they called me outside. They were in the walnut tree in our backyard."

Patterson rolled his eyes, then tried to smile. "They were in the walnut tree in our backyard?"

Ledyard didn't smile. "Yes!"

"Now come on, Ledyard, don't that sound a might far-fetched to you? Invisible folks in our walnut tree? Callin' you outside and talkin' to you?"

"They've come around more than a few times since, daddy," Ledyard intoned.

"In the walnut tree?"

"No, not in the walnut tree! I don't know why they picked the walnut tree the first time. Maybe they were just seein' if I would respond to their coaxin', to get me ready for an out-of-body experience or somethin'."

"An out-of-body experience!" his father puffed. "Ledyard, what on Earth are you talkin' about?"

"Well, I've been tryin' to tell you, daddy, but you just won't listen. Just the other night when they came and told me about Mohammed bein' in heaven and how Jesus is a friend of his...."

"Mohammed, a friend of Jesus!?" his father exploded.

"Yes," Ledyard insisted. "I've been tryin' to tell y'all...."

"Jesus is *not* a friend of Mohammed!" the reverend roared. "Christians and Moslems have been at war for over a thousand years!"

"I know, and it's wrong," Ledyard said firmly.

"Wrong? Are you crazy, boy? Moslem's have been fightin' the work of Christ since Mohammed founded his rogue religion some 1300 years ago. They're doin' the work of Satan. And now, apparently, so are you. Or at least you c'ain't wait to try your hand at it!"

"What makes you so sure they're doin' the work of Satan?"

"Because they reject Christ! And John 14:6 says...."

"I know what John 14:6 says," Ledyard snapped. "But how do you know that Mohammed wasn't moved by God for some purpose of God's that we have no idea of? How do you know Mohammed isn't in heaven right now havin' done well in God's eyes? If so it would mean that John 14:6 don't automatically rule out Moslems, or any other religious group for that matter!"

"You sure have twisted that one around!" his father snarled.

"I haven't twisted anything!" Ledyard heatedly declared. "I'm simply tellin' y'all what they told me!"

At that the reverend's face grew ominously dark and his eyes narrowed. "Do you realize what you're sayin' to me?" he asked softly, then continued without waiting for an answer. "You're tellin' me that you're receivin' direct revelation from God. Yet everything you've confronted me with in the last several years has been a direct contradiction of the scriptures as I understand them!"

Ledyard lowered his eyes. "I know," he almost whispered.

"Right. Now, who do you think has a better understandin' of God and the scriptures? You, with 14 years experience on this Earth, or me, with 39?"

"But daddy, I'm not claimin' to understand anything. I'm just tellin' you what I've been told by somethin' that's out there," he gestured at the ceiling.

"That's what's so disturbin' to me, Ledyard. You're claimin' direct revelation from God. Do you suppose yourself to be a prophet?"

Speechless, Ledyard stared at him.

"Well do you? Because if you persist in claimin' to receive revelation from heaven, well then you are, in fact, claimin' to be a prophet of God. Are you prepared to back up that claim? Would you like to step into my pulpit come Sunday?"

"No, daddy," Ledyard shook his head. "I swear, I'm not claimin' to be a prophet, I'm just tellin' y'all...."

"No!" his father thundered, "you c'ain't have it both ways! Either you are a prophet, receivin' direct revelation from heaven, or you're not. Now which is it?"

Ledyard stared long and hard at some distant point. Suddenly he brightened, turning to his father. "No! Don't you get it?" he exclaimed, "you're the preacher, you're the prophet. They're just usin' me to reach you!"

At that his father burst out laughing. "Yeah, right Ledyard. Sure. I'm supposed to get on international television and start preachin' the nonsense you've been relatin' to me?" After his laughter subsided he continued in a darkly serious tone. "You know what I think, Ledyard? I think you're either mildly schizophrenic and experiencin' hallucinations or," he shook his head sadly, "somehow you've become in league with Satan."

"In league with Satan? Why, because I disagree with you? Is everyone who disagrees with you in league with Satan?"

His father slowly nodded. "I'm afraid so, boy. You see, I know my master's voice. I know when God speaks to me, directs me in what to teach in my sermons. And in fact there is not one single solitary Christian theologian, minister, scholar, whatever, who would agree with you that Moslems go to heaven. And if you really believe you received *that* revelation from God then I'm afraid you're either a very sick boy or your God is Satan."

"Yeah?" Ledyard hotly retorted and leaped to his feet. "How do you know *your* revelations aren't from Satan?"

"Because *I'm* doin' the work of Christ!" his father said indignantly, also getting to his feet.

"You and your seed-faith," Ledyard spat the words, "when the Bible abounds with warnin's as to the dangers and evils of materialism! As if God was concerned with how much money a person has in his pockets. You're not doin' the work of Christ, you're short-circuitin' the work of Christ!"

At that the reverend slapped his son a stinging crack across the face. Putting a hand to his cheek in disbelief, Ledyard made a move to leave but his father blocked his path. Raising his voice to the ceiling, the reverend bellowed so loudly the lampshades trembled, "GRANGER! GRANGER, GET DOWN HERE THIS INSTANT!"

To Ledyard he ordered sharply, "Sit down!"

Staring at him, Ledyard slowly sank to the couch.

"I c'ain't have you goin' to that rally in your condition. There's liable to be press showin' up. That's all I need, to have you blathering your idiotic hallucinations to them!"

At that moment Granger rushed into the room looking very concerned. "Yes sir?"

Waving a finger at Ledyard, the reverend said, "This boy is not to leave the house this evenin' for any reason. Do you understand?"

"Yes sir," Granger answered, glancing at Ledyard curiously.

Once again he turned on his son. "We are not finished, young man. I'm a goin' to get your soul right with God if it's the last thing I do!" And with that he stormed from the room.

Keeping an eye on Ledyard, Granger slowly sank to the edge of one easy chair. A self-conscious smile on his face, he shrugged as if to say none of what happened was any of his doing.

To his surprise Ledyard smiled back. After a moment the boy leaned forward, elbows on his knees, and asked quietly, "Can God do anything, Mr. Granger?"

Granger shrugged. "Far as I know."

With a sly grin Ledyard slowly shook his head. "No, Granger. Sometimes God c'ain't even answer a simple prayer."

"Oh?" Granger said with interest, sliding back in the easy chair and putting his feet up. "How's that, Ledyard?" he asked, deciding to humor this obviously disturbed and spoiled rich kid.

"I'll tell you how," Ledyard said with a bemused smile. "The people are in the church on Wednesday evenin', okay?"

Granger nodded once. "Okay."

"And the minister asks the people to pray that God grant a sunny day for the comin' Saturday, which is the day of the church picnic, okay?"

Again Granger nodded. "Okay."

"But by Friday all the farmers in four states are realizin' that one more hot, dry day and the spring planting will be ruined, and go to bed prayin' for a good rain." Ledyard paused. "Whose prayer is God goin' to answer?"

"Well, that's simple, Ledyard, the farmer's prayer, of course, because it's more important."

"That may well be, Granger, but then he *c'ain't* answer the simple prayer of the church group, now can he?"

*   *   *

Getting into his pajamas for bed that evening, Ledyard was praying. He prayed to God for the Invisible Ones to return. To give him another chance. If only they would come back and try their thing again, this time, he vowed, he wouldn't fight it. This time, in the name of Jesus, he would go with them.

As soon as his head hit the pillow and he closed his eyes he was put to the test. Again it came on rapidly: a mounting pressure, a tingling paralysis enveloping his entire body, a steadily growing rushing sound roaring in his head. And then, as if a giant vacuum cleaner nozzle were poised directly above him, the incredible pulling sensation of something trying to suck him up into... where?

With a pounding heart he remembered his vow of only seconds before and fervently prayed for Jesus to protect his soul, while consciously fighting the urge to resist the powerful force that seemed to be trying to suck him right out of himself and right out of bed!

Yet armed with unshakable faith in God and the knowledge that he could apparently "kill" the experience at any time, he managed to take a deep breath, relax, and give himself over to the tremendous powers that were suffocatingly pulling at him from all sides.

It happened so fast, the acceleration so rapid, that all he saw were the attic rafters flashing by before he was outside in the dark streaking towards the stars, the twinkling lights of Houston far below.

Triumphantly exhilarated, the cool night air rushing through him sweeping away all fear, he started checking out his body. He was dumbfounded as he stared at his hand. He couldn't *see* it, but it was there. He flexed his fingers, feeling as though he could grasp something if there had been something to grasp. And his knee. He put his hand on his knee and could *feel* it. But that motion also sent him tumbling and he stretched out flat in an instinctive effort to control it. And that's when he noticed. He was alone. But only seconds ago there had been others. Invisible Ones. Where were they?

All at once he looked around and in a moment of fear and confusion as to which way was up and which way was down, which were the stars and which were the twinkling

lights of the city, he experienced a sudden dread fear of getting lost in space and cried out to dear God to be home.

And he was. Physical. Lying in his bed. He sat up staring wide-eyed in the dark, heart pounding. Was he insane?

CLOUD DROPS

13

FUN UNDER THE SON

> *That which hath been is now; and that which is to be hath already been....*
> *- ECCLESIASTES 3:15*

Since Cambian was scheduled to appear before the House of Kings the following morning to give a progress report, and with the "kids" already having departed with the orientation team which would instruct them in the ways and means of heaven, the whole rescue squad had the day off. At poolside over a breakfast of strawberries and cream they were discussing what to do with their free time. Everyone wanted to do something different.

Avery and his girlfriends were going down to the ocean on the extreme western edge of Greasy City to do a little offshore powerboat racing. On their last outing Georgia had placed first in the first race, Loretta had taken first in the second race, and Anna had placed first in the third race. In all three races Avery's best had been third place in the second race. In the third he flipped the boat at a 115 mph, totally demolishing the craft. Ruled "dead" by the judges, he was excluded from the final two races and would have to return on another day to try again. Now the competition among the girls was really hot to see who could keep him from claiming the number one spot.

James and his four girlfriends also had a stiff racing competition going, but on Greasy City's Grand Prix circuit, which came with a complete replication of the race course at Monaco. James was running a Lotus, Pauline a Ferrari, Alison a Maserati, Margaret a Lamborghini, and Eileen a Porsche. Various other contestants would be running similar vehicles.

James and the girls tried talking Cambian and his mates into joining them in a racing competition, but to no avail. Debbie, Natalie, and Michelle had made up their minds weeks ago; at the first opportunity they were going south and hiring a 65-foot Trimaran sailboat to do some diving in the clear, blue-green waters off the coast, play with some dolphins, and maybe get a ride on a whale's back. It sounded like a pretty good idea to Cambian, too.

Andy and his three girls were heading off to a ski lodge in the mountains up north for a little deep-powder skiing. That they only had a day and 3,000 miles to cover was irrelevant when they could travel at thought-speed and arrive in a thousandth of a second.

Since everyone was anxious to be off, after breakfast they simply snapped away the dirty dishes and assembled on the front lawn. Waving goodbye to each other, the four "mini teams" lifted off and went their separate ways.

*   *   *

Arriving at the seaport town of Regina Cove on the southern coast, Cambian "radioed" from the air as to the availability of any Trimaran sailing yachts for hire. He received an immediate reply that three were available for the choosing. One was a 65-footer. Exactly what they were looking for. Cambian requested a locator beacon.

Far below a light flashed from a large victorian house tucked in a cove on the beach east of town. "That's our boat," Cambian said as they plummeted for the ground.

They landed on the front lawn as a thirty-ish looking man with long, white-blond hair and a body bronzed from the sun, a woman of similar age and appearance, and two teenage boys came out on the porch to greet them. "Aye, kids!" the man called with a wave. "Out for a little rest and relaxation, eh?"

"Yes, sir!" Cambian grinned, snapping off a salute.

"Well the boat's all stocked and ready," he called, "come on up and meet the crew."

Although there was no such thing as marriage in the Earthly sense, it was not uncommon for families to reunite when, or if, they all made it to heaven. This was one such family.

As Cambian and the girls gained the porch the man stuck a hand out and introduced himself. "Name's Charley Sutton," he said, taking Cambian's hand in a firm grip. "And this is my wife, Belinda, and my two sons, Karl and Kevin." Everyone shook hands as Cambian and the girls introduced themselves.

"We were hoping someone would come by," Charley grinned, adding, "beautiful day for an outing!"

Everyone agreed. "Well, let's get started then," he said, leading the way down the steps and across the beach to the wooden pier where the gleaming white 65-foot trimaran was docked.

"Beautiful boat!" Natalie exclaimed as they tromped down the pier.

"We sure like her," Charlie said, jumping into the cock-pit and turning to give his wife a hand. Karl and Kevin jumped on the bow, Cambian and the girls following suit. Once everyone was aboard Belinda turned to the three girls and said, "Let me show you the cabin while these guys get us launched."

As they climbed down the companionway into the cabin the girls heard the little diesel motor sputter to life and their host call out, "Cast off the bowline, Kevin!" A moment later the engine clunked into gear, the boat trembling briefly as it started to move away from the pier.

The sumptuous main cabin had a galley with refrigerator, stove, double sink, plenty of storage space, and a lounge with place-settings for ten. The head was only a vanity with sink and shower stall as there was no need for a commode. The spacious aft stateroom was the host and hostess's personal quarters. Two comfortable forward cabins with double bunks were for guests.

From above they heard Charley's shouts to man the halyard and raise the sail; the whir of lines being pulled and a moment later, the snap of the sail unfurling and catching the breeze. "Watch it, spar's coming 'round!"

Turning to Natalie and Michelle, Debbie exclaimed, "I just love it! Aren't you glad we decided to do this?" Giddy with excitement and a sense of adventure, both her companions readily agreed.

By the time the girls emerged from the cabin the boat was out of the harbor and crashing through the waves with gathering speed. Bouncing up and down on the bow-netting like two kids on a trampoline, Cambian and Kevin were yelling "Yahooo!" with the salty spray of every swell the bow burst through.

"Let's set for a port tack," the skipper said to his eldest son, Karl.

"Right, dad," the boy replied and set to work making the proper adjustments. They were on a course bearing north-by-northwest, the coastline off the starboard side.

With all the girls crowded into the cockpit the skipper took the opportunity to ask, "Did you ladies have anything special in mind that you wanted to do today?"

"Could we go skin diving off the barrier reef?" Debbie asked hopefully.

"And play with some dolphins?" Natalie put in.

"And get a ride on a whale's back!" Michelle cried excitedly.

Charley laughed. "Wow, it sounds like we're going to have a pretty busy day! But yes," he added, "I think we can get all of that in."

"Yea!" the girls cheered.

With the boys bouncing around on the bow-netting, the girls clambered onto the starboard wing-net and lay down in a row on their bellies, watching the crystal clear water racing beneath them and bursting out with laughter every time they lost their stomachs when the boat rose on a swell and dropped into a trough.

Once Karl had the sails trimmed just right he dropped into the port wing-net with a bounce and lay on his back, hands folded behind his head, the girls just visible over the cabin roof.

When Debbie craned her neck for a chance peek back, sky-blue eyes dancing, long blond hair hanging almost to her butt, he quickly looked away. "I think that boy likes you, Natalie," she giggled. "I saw him looking at you when we were standing on the pier."

"Which one?" Natalie asked, emerald-green eyes alight to match the jade beads that held her dreadlocks.

"The oldest, Karl."

"I wouldn't kick him out for eatin' kippers and crackers in bed," Natalie grinned, tossing aside her dreadlocks and looking back over one brown shoulder. When she did he caught her eye and smiled. She turned back to her friends. "I know who *I'm* sleepin' with tonight!"

"Then I get Kevin!" Michelle laughed, her bright-orange, shiny, straight pixie-cut hair almost glowing in the sun.

Kevin looked up from where he and Cambian had ceased their bouncing and were comparing big toes. He grinned and gave her a wink.

This threw the girls into a fit of giggling, a red-faced Michelle exclaiming in mock mortification, "Oh my God he heard me!"

"Look there, off the port side!" Charley suddenly cried and pointed, "Dolphins!"

Everyone turned to look, the girls sitting up, then standing. A school of dolphins were rising and plunging in perfect harmony as they paced the boat. "Watch it," the skipper called, "I'm gonna bring 'er 'round and see if they follow."

As he guided the boat into a westerly course the dolphins, maintaining perfect formation, followed suit. After a moment Charley called out, "Karl, prepare to man the halyard and lower the sail!"

"Aye-aye!" Karl called back and took his station.

"Heads up, everyone!" the skipper called out the warning. Once to windward Karl quickly lowered the sail.

As the sailboat died in the water and began to drift the dolphins noticed and doubled back. Playfully leaping and diving off the port side, one flipped up on its tail and skittered backwards across the water, nodding its head and crying with happy chatter for the kids to come for a swim.

"Can we?" Natalie turned to Charley.

"Why not?" he shrugged.

Immediately the girls scrambled over the cabin to the port side, whipped off their shorts and dove into the sea. Taking it all in, Cambian was excitedly running back and forth on the cabin roof, then leaped to the netting, bounced into the air and out of his shorts and dove in after the girls. The Sutton boys stood watching for a moment, laughing at the antics of their guests, then stripped and dove in too.

They played with the dolphins for over an hour until Charley and Belinda, watching from a perch on the port outrigger, wondered who would tire first, the kids or the dolphins. At last, though, they all climbed out of the water and flopped down on the netting to rest and warm themselves in the sun.

With his wife assisting, the skipper raised the sail and called out as they got under way, "Still want to explore the barrier reef?"

"Yes!" came the unanimous cry.

After a brief nap they arrived at the barrier reef rested and ready and once again dove into the water. Unimpeded by physical limitations, they could remain underwater indefinitely without aqualungs, and they explored the undersea wonders for hours. When at last Michelle popped to the surface, Charley called out, "If you want to see the whales we'd better get under way because they're out in the deep water and there's only a few hours of daylight left."

Michelle immediately "radioed" her companions and everyone popped to the surface and climbed aboard. Then Charley put out for the high seas.

Two hours later, with the coast but a thin green line on the horizon, they still hadn't spotted any whales. Reading the disappointment on Michelle's face, Charley asked his wife to take the helm, stood up and announced, "Well, I guess I'd better try my whale call."

With Cambian and the girls curiously looking on and his two sons sporting knowing grins, Charley climbed onto the starboard wing-net and lay on his stomach near the edge. With Karl holding onto his ankles, he plunged head-first into the water and made the thin, almost soundless cry of the whales. After several minutes of this he pulled out of the water and lay back on the netting.

"Do you think it'll work?" Michelle asked.

He smiled and nodded. "I think so. Just keep your eye off the bow." With that he rolled to his knees, got up and returned to the helm.

"Wow," Michelle exclaimed with admiration, "it's not everyone that can talk to whales!" And then she joined the others on the bow-net where they sat on the edge with their feet dangling over the side. Occasionally someone would shade their eyes with a hand and shout excitedly, "I think I see one!"

Charley laughed and hollered from the stern, "Don't worry, you'll know it when you do!"

And then they did. Not 20 feet off the starboard bow a massive monster 150-feet long and 40-feet tall rose from the waves, the sailboat beside it bobbing in the water like a toy. With the glistening orb of one eye warily watching them, it blew a huge geyser into the air. Then, plunging for the depths, it sent a wave crashing over the trimaran, the water rolling off the cabin roof and cascading through the hatch.

With fear and wonder the kids impulsively leapt to their feet and stampeded for the cockpit. Laughing with delight, Charley asked, "Still want to ride one, Michelle?"

Michelle looked at him like he was crazy. "No way!" she exclaimed, "there wouldn't be any way to hang on!"

"Sure there's a way." They all looked up to see Cambian standing above them on the cabin roof.

"How?" Michelle wanted to know.

"Simple," Cambian answered. "With these." He looked down at his hands. A second later there was a *pfhht!* and he was sporting rubber suction cups strapped to his hands and feet.

Michelle eyed him for a moment making sure he was serious, then looked down at her own hands. A second later *pfhht!* and she was wearing identical suction cups.

Natalie and Debbie both looked at her, exclaiming in unison, "You're crazy, girl!"

With a grin Cambian reached down, took Michelle's hand and pulled her up beside him. "You game?"

She rolled her eyes and laughed, saying, "One of these days, boy!" And then hand-in-hand they made their way to the bow.

At that moment a second whale, perhaps the first whale's mate, rose up, towering over them. "Come on!" Cambian yelled.

Still holding hands, they leaped into the water and started swimming furiously for the beast. But they didn't have to swim for very long, for as it started its plunge it sucked them both right to its side where they slammed the cups against its glistening blue-gray hide. Thus attached and looking like twin Captain Ahab's but without the harpoon ropes crisscrossing their bodies, they plunged beneath the waves and were gone.

"Coming 'round!" Charley cried as he spun the wheel to give chase. And then they were racing with the wind, crashing through wave after wave as the mighty whales rose like mountains out of the sea, plunging and rising again and again, the two tiny figures of Michelle and Cambian clinging to the one whale's side.

As Debbie and Natalie joined the two Sutton boys at the bow, Karl remarked with awe and admiration, "I've never seen anyone do anything like that before!"

"Had enough?" Cambian shouted to Michelle as they exploded to the surface. They'd been riding the whale for some 30 minutes at this point.

Grinning from ear-to-ear, Michelle nodded. "Let's go!"

Just as the whale reached the peak of its arc, in a snap the suction cups were gone and in one motion the two turned and pushed off the side with their feet, doing swan dives as they splashed into the water some 40 feet below.

Within minutes the trimaran was bearing down on them, Karl and Kevin hanging over the starboard side and sweeping them aboard as the yacht raced by.

"Had enough of whale riding, did ya?" a grinning Charley asked, the two dripping adventurers trembling with chill and pumping adrenaline as they jumped into the cockpit.

"You bet!" Michelle laughed as she and Cambian ducked into the cabin for a hot shower and a warm blanket.

"Well, what say we put in for a cove and hide out for the night?" Charley asked the rest of his crew.

Everyone thought it was a great idea.

CLOUD DROPS

14

THE MORE THE MERRIER

> *All the rivers run into the sea; yet the sea is not full; unto the place from whence the rivers come, thither they return again.*
> *- ECCLESIASTES 1:7*

The sky was a fiery-red when they dropped anchor in a sandy little cove sheltered by a crescent of beach dotted with tall palm trees rustling in the warm tropical breeze. Beyond the beach was a thick tangle of dark, emerald-green jungle filled with the cawing, hooting screeches of nocturnal creatures just awakening for the night's hunt. In the crimson darkness warm yellow light glowed from the yacht's windows.

Inside the cozy little cabin Debbie was lighting the stove while Michelle was banging pots and pans in search of a skillet for frying the ocean perch caught earlier.

At the table Charley, Belinda, Natalie, Cambian, Karl and Kevin were engaged in a rather loud and raucous game of cards. "King of diamonds!" Cambian cried, slapping the card down with a flourish.

"Hey! I thought that was already played," Kevin protested.

Grinning mischievously, Cambian shook his head, "Nope."

"That's all right," Charley said with a wink and flipped the two of spades onto the table, "I'll take it with this." To Cambian he commented, "You hung on to that one too long, son."

Cambian grimaced. Natalie laughed, her large green eyes sparkling against her dark, silky-smooth skin as she exclaimed, "He always does that!"

From the galley came the sizzle of fish hitting the fry pan and Michelle calling, "Asparagus in butter sauce all right with everyone?"

"Great!"

"Wonderful!"

"Sounds good to me!" came a chorus of voices.

"What's that bring the score to now, honey?" Charley asked his wife, designated official scorekeeper and now frowning over her figures, the pencil in her teeth.

She removed the pencil and did some more figuring. "Let's see. That puts me in the lead, Charley second, Natalie third, and it's a close race between Kevin, Cambian, and Karl."

The boys groaned, Karl saying impatiently, "Okay, deal the cards!"

"Hold that deal!" Debbie called and came to the table with a platter of crisp hot perch, a little smoke plume curling off. "Dinner is served!" Michelle was right behind her with a sterling platter of steaming, lightly salted buttered asparagus.

"Sure smells good!" Charley exclaimed, sweeping the cards off the table as his wife reached for a stack of plates and silverware on the counter.

Debbie and Michelle set their platters in the center of the table and sat down as Belinda passed plates and utensils to everyone.

"You girls sure know how to cook," Karl said, digging in.

"And how!" Kevin enthusiastically agreed.

Debbie and Michelle fairly glowed with pride, Cambian adding, "Best cooks on the whole team."

Helping herself to a serving of asparagus, Belinda said, "You guys are part of a rescue squad on Earth duty, aren't you?"

"How'd you know?" Michelle asked.

"The shorts," Belinda replied, "all the same with the little symbol on the hip. Besides," she added, "we were on a rescue squad once, too."

"How's the rescue business going these days?" Charley asked, popping a morsel of crisp fish into his mouth.

Cambian shrugged. "It has its moments. You know, watching the world evolve from the sky, seeing strange and exotic places like America. Working with the kids." He paused, spearing an asparagus with his fork. "But I've been at it for quite awhile now. I think when I get done with this special project I'm working on I'm going to take some time off and do a little exploring." He glanced at the girls. "That is if I can get Debbie, Natalie, and Michelle to come along."

"How old are you?" Charley asked.

"Well, let's see," Cambian answered, counting on his fingers, "46."

"May I ask how…."

"Vietnam. A casualty when the war moved into Cambodia in '68."

There was a momentary lapse of silence, the only sound being the clink and clatter of silverware. Finally Cambian looked up. "How about yourself?"

"Normandy, 1944," Charley answered.

"We got lucky, though," Belinda intoned. "Less than a year later, in '45, a truck pulled out in front of us on a highway in New Jersey and me and the boys were killed instantly."

"Wow, that was lucky," Debbie put in.

"So you guys have been together for quite some time," Cambian said.

"Well..." Charley raised his eyes to the ceiling, mentally counting. "Yes, we met in high school in '33 when we were both 16, married in '37," he paused, concluding, "66 years, not counting the brief interruption between '43 and '45." He turned to his wife, "And that makes us...."

"Eighty-two," she answered for him. "And that makes Karl 62 and Kevin 61."

"Wow!" Debbie exclaimed, "you guys have been together for a long time!"

"That we have, lass, and loving every minute of it," Charley said, adding, "and how about yourselves?"

"I've been with the rescue squad four years," Debbie answered. "Just turned 20 last month. Died in an air crash flying home from a European vacation."

Natalie and Karl, making eyes at one another and playing footsie under the table, were caught off guard when everyone turned on her expectantly. "What?" she asked, looking around the table.

"Charley was asking how old we are," Michelle informed her, "and it's just gotten 'round to you."

"Oh. I'm 12. Joined the rescue squad when I was five."

"Five!" Belinda exclaimed, "that seems awfully young!"

Natalie laughed. "Not really. I'd already been here just a little less than five years when I joined."

Karl looked at her in wonder. "Well you must have been...."

"Crib death," she answered, "three months old."

"Oh!" everyone laughed, "that explains it!"

Then everyone looked at Michelle. "Seventy-eight," she answered. "Been with the squad three years. Expired of natural causes. Heart failure. I suspect too much red meat, eggs, and cheese!" she laughed.

Everyone applauded, Belinda commenting, "Well it's nice to hear that *somebody* made it of natural causes!"

"So how long have you guys been running this charter service?" Cambian asked.

"Oh, let's see, we were all with a rescue squad for what, 20 years?" Charley turned to his wife questioningly.

"That's right, from '46 to '66."

"Then we retired here and started the charter service. Been at it ever since."

"You must like it," Cambian said.

"We *love* it," Belinda corrected.

"For me it was a lifelong dream realized," Charley said. "And we meet all sorts of interesting people. Why, we even had Abraham Lincoln and Robert E. Lee as guests once!"

"And we've sailed all over Universe Center several times," Belinda put in.

"And still have a dozen more places we want to visit," Charley said. "And if we ever get bored with it," he shrugged, "well, I understand there's about ten zillion planets out there to explore in this great big wide open universe of ours."

"And ten zillion more in the second universe," Kevin put in.

"And ten zillion more in the third," Cambian laughed.

"And so on and so on," Michelle grinned.

After their laughter abated, Charley got to his feet, saying conclusively, "Well, I don't know about you guys but I'm beat." Turning to his wife he asked, "Ready to turn in, honey?"

She nodded, taking his hand and letting him pull her to her feet where they retired to the aft stateroom.

After they were gone Karl turned to Natalie. "Would you like to sleep under the stars tonight?"

"That sounds like a wonderful idea," Natalie said, getting to her feet and peering up at the sky through the companionway. "It looks like a beautiful night for it, too."

"I'll get some blankets and pillows," Karl said, going to a storage closet.

"Get some for us, too," Cambian said, "I think Debbie and I will join you."

"And us, too," Kevin put in, glancing at Michelle, who smiled and nodded.

"Great," Karl grinned, "the more the merrier." Then he turned back to rummaging for blankets.

With blankets and pillows in hand the three couples filed through the companionway and out onto the deck under a velvet-black sky shimmering with billions of stars. The balmy summer night air was filled with the fragrance of tropical breezes, the trimaran rocking gently as small waves lapped against the hull.

"I think we can all fit comfortably on the bow-net," Karl said softly, taking Natalie by the hand and leading the way.

With Michelle and Kevin taking the middle, Natalie and Karl were on one side, Cambian and Debbie on the other.

"I don't remember what the planet is called," Cambian was saying to Debbie as they snuggled beneath the blankets, "I'll have to go back to the library and look it up again."

"What're you guys talking about?" Michelle asked.

Feeling the warmth of Michelle at his back, Cambian answered over his shoulder, "Debbie doesn't know if she's going to go with us when I get done with the mission."

"Why not, Deb?"

"Because I'm worried about my parents and sister coming out when I'm gone and missing them," Debbie answered.

"I think you guys are discussing this a little prematurely," Michelle replied. "I mean, Cambian's still got to touch down, and once he does he might end up spending 40, 50, or even a hundred years down there. By then, Deb, your parents will either be here or they won't. And besides," she added, "even if you did miss them you could always catch up with them later. I don't see what the problem is."

Michelle turned back to Kevin, who had thrown off the blanket and was already transforming to receive her and burn-off the night's spectacular dinner with a night of spectacular lovemaking. They were a perfect match.

Drawing Debbie into a tight embrace, Cambian said softly, "See? We're worrying about this for nothing."

Heaving a sigh, Debbie looked at him and smiled. "Yes, I suppose you're right."

*   *   *

The next morning Cambian explained to his hosts that they had to be back directly and wouldn't be returning to Regina Cove on the yacht.

"Could I come with you?" Karl asked.

"Me too?" Kevin put in, "just for a day or two until you leave on your next mission?"

Cambian looked at the girls. They grinned and nodded enthusiastically. "Well, if it's okay with Natalie and Michelle then it's okay with me."

"Can we, dad?" Karl asked, turning to his father.

He shrugged, "I don't see why not. Your mother and I can handle the boat."

"Then we'd better be off," Cambian said, turning to Belinda with an embrace and a kiss. "Thanks for a wonderful time."

"You're quite welcome," she said.

He turned to the skipper, likewise embracing him. "And thank you, Charley, it was great."

"Come back and see us any time," Charley smiled warmly.

After the girls hugged and kissed their hosts goodbye the team and their guests gathered in a circle on the bow, joined hands and lifted off for the sky and home.

Approaching the City of Kings, they slowed, then stopped, hovering over the stately, pillared House of Kings, Natalie explaining to Karl and Kevin that they were dropping Cambian off.

"Well, bye everyone," Cambian said, "and I'll see you at the house later."

"Okay," Debbie replied, "we'll be waiting for you."

"Great, see you then," he said and dropped from the "ship."

At the House of Kings Jesus was just introducing Cambian when the boy pulled the door open and entered. In the foyer he paused until the Lord was finished, then stepped into the rotunda before the gathered forum.

"And what do you have to report?" Jesus asked, putting a friendly arm around his shoulders.

"We've had a great success," Cambian answered, speaking to the audience at large. "We finally drew him out of his body."

At that everyone applauded.

"And what effect do you think this will have?" Mohammed called from his seat.

"Well," Cambian weighed his words carefully, "I think originally he had a real fear that we might somehow be connected with evil. Now, as a result of his brief but harmless out-of-body experience I believe he's beginning to develop some real trust." Cambian paused. "But he's also beginning to experience some real difficulties on the home front, too."

"Which tells us that he *is* bringing up the points that you and your team have been feeding him telepathically," Jesus intoned.

"Absolutely," Cambian declared. "In fact he's doing more than that—he's *arguing* them. But, as I said, he is experiencing some real difficulties at home and it seems to be getting worse."

"Meaning?" Jesus pleasantly inquired.

Cambian turned to him. "Meaning that I think it's time for a visitation. To sort of fortify him once and for all for the long haul he's eventually going to be confronted with."

"Hmmm," Jesus pondered.

"I just feel it's the next logical step before touching down," Cambian added.

Jesus paced about for a moment, deep in thought, then looked up and sighed. "Yes, I suppose you're right." He turned to the forum at large and spoke loudly, "How do all of you feel about this? Anyone like to give us some input or ask a question?"

No one did, Martin Luther King commenting, "I think we all understand the situation."

After Jesus put the proposal to a vote and received a unanimous response in the affirmative he turned to Cambian and said, "Well, good luck young man. And keep up the good work."

Cambian bowed and said, "Thank you, my Lord," then turned to the assembly and bowed again, thanking them as well.

CLOUD DROPS

15

A MOMENTARY LAPSE OF FAITH

> *Therefore pray not thou for this people, neither lift up cry nor prayer for them, neither make intercession to me: for I will not hear thee.*
>
> *- JEREMIAH 7:16*

The big game on Friday night had the Christian Condensed Angels on the gridiron hunkering down against the Prophets from Methodist Saint Matthew's High in Houston. For the first time in two weeks, after Ledyard had experienced a series of disasters, the coach thought the boy ready for another chance and sent him in as wide receiver.

The first quarter went well for the Angels, ending with a score of 14 - 0, Ledyard making the run for the second touchdown. The second quarter had the Prophets tying up the game with two touchdowns of their own, a fierce drive that came after the coach pulled Ledyard to give his second stringer a try. He dropped a perfect pass.

When the halftime horn sounded, Ledyard trotted for the locker room with the other boys. Inside, they dropped wearily to the benches, heads hanging, surprised at how tired they were. They had been playing hard.

The coach, pacing up and down, waited until everyone had caught their breath, then said evenly, "Y'all were killin' 'em the first quarter. What happened?" He looked at Roger.

"Well don't look at me!" Roger protested indignantly, "I didn't drop the perfect pass, I threw it!"

"All right, Roger," the coach held up a hand and turned to the team in general. Hesitating for just an instant, he began solemnly, "Boys, when we first gathered in this room did I sense a momentary lapse of faith?" His hard stare moved around the room. "Is that what was happening out on the field during the second quarter?"

No one said a word.

"All right, look," he began again, softening somewhat, "I know y'all got it in you. The Prophets just got a handle on our battle plan quicker than we thought." Suddenly sprouting a grin, he shrugged. "So? Now we switch to plan 'B.' What could be simpler?"

Greatly relieved, the Sophomore team grinned back, raised their fists in the air and chanted, "Three cheers for coach Crawford! HEY! HEY! HEY!"

"Thank you, boys. Okay, I'll make this quick and let y'all relax for a minute. Let's pray."

All the boys joined hands and bowed their heads. "Lord Jesus, I beseech thee, bless this ministry's team...."

As the coach rambled on, Roger kept a discreet eye on Ledyard to his immediate right, the best friend whose warm, moist hand he now held in prayer—or at least in what *appeared* to be praying.

"Thank you, Lord Jesus," Coach Crawford concluded.

As the boys let go hands and raised their heads Roger said evenly, "Ledyard weren't prayin' with us, he was thinkin' about somethin' else."

"You're right, Roger, I *was* thinkin' about somethin' else," Ledyard responded immediately. "I was thinkin' how odd that y'all should imagine God bein' interested in the outcome of our petty little football game."

Someone coughed.

Someone else said, "We were gonna make this short."

The coach took two steps towards Ledyard, peered at him darkly, then said, "Bad attitude."

No one thought to ask Roger what *he'd* been thinking about during prayer.

For the third quarter Ledyard was benched, the coach wanting to give his second stringer another chance. On faith. And the boy, overly anxious to make good, promptly dropped his second perfect pass of the evening. Then, with only seconds to go the Prophets scored a field goal, ending the third quarter with a score of 17 - 14 in their favor.

Facing the fourth quarter, things were hot and heavy and the coach put Ledyard back in. It had been a tough, tight game that had spectators in the bleachers on both sides of the field roaring their disappointment one moment and wildly cheering and stomping their feet the next.

Fiercely determined to stop the other, neither team was making much headway. Then the Angels broke through and scored a touchdown but missed the extra point, bringing the score to 20 - 17 in their favor. Shortly thereafter, on their last down, the Prophets successfully went for the field goal, tying up the game for a second time.

With less than a minute to go in the final quarter the spectators were roaring a chant, their pounding feet creating a thundering rhythm as the Angel's center hiked the ball. The quarterback dropped back, hesitated as a defensive tackle slipped around a guard, then at the last possible moment fired off a pass to Ledyard, who caught the ball smack in the midriff, spun and ran 40 yards for the winning touchdown.

The Prophets hadn't time to get off a play before the horn sounded ending the game and signaling an Angel victory. With the Angel spectators wildly cheering, Ledyard's teammates hoisted him to their shoulders and carried him off the field where they were engulfed by a gaggle of press on the sidelines: a reporter and photographer from the high school paper as well as a team from the college paper, a radio sports reporter and one from the college TV station. Granger was also there, inconspicuously at the fringe of the crowd.

"What a fantastic play!" the radio reporter exclaimed, shoving a microphone in Ledyard's face as soon as his teammates set him down. "How does it feel after being sidelined for two weeks?"

"Great!" Ledyard grinned, "but I only caught the pass. Why don't y'all talk to the man who threw it?"

Then he attempted to duck out for the locker room, but another reporter managed to block his escape and he was quickly surrounded again. "I noticed you sitting with your head bowed right before your fabulous fourth-quarter play. Were you praying for help?"

"No I weren't prayin' for help. I was restin'."

"So you don't believe praying before a game has any merit?"

Ledyard chuckled, "Any merit? No, I think it's right silly."

"So you don't feel God played any role in the success of this game?" the reporter persisted.

About to shove through and be on his way, Ledyard stopped, eyeing the reporter and saying, "Let's put the question another way."

"Okay," the reporter bobbed his head once.

"Do y'all believe God had any role in the *failure* of the Prophets to win?" Then he shoved through the crowd and strode quickly for the locker room, the pursuing press excitedly shouting questions after him.

In the shower room Roger deliberately sought a spot next to Ledyard. Stepping under the hot stream and leaning forward slightly to let it pound on his aching shoulder, he said, "Why'd ya do it?"

"What?" Ledyard inquired mildly, his annoyance over the locker room betrayal at halftime tempered by the fact that it had given him an opportunity to boldly express his views.

Roger was surprised. He had expected some resentment at least. "Say what you said to the press," he glanced at Ledyard. "You *know* what the headline's gonna read tomorrow mornin'."

"Oh? What?"

"That Ledyard Patterson doesn't believe in the power of prayer!" he exclaimed. "Or somethin' like it, anyway."

"But that's *not* what I said," Ledyard countered.

"Well it sure sounded like that to me." Roger turned slightly to let the pounding stream massage another area. "And I'll tell ya somethin' else, Ledyard, me and you been friends for what, almost three years now? And your unpopular views are beginnin' to rub even *me* the wrong way."

"What're ya sayin', Roger?" Ledyard asked, eyeing him.

"I'm sayin' you're startin' to lose friends, Led. Every time you turn around you're attacking our beliefs. And when I say *our* beliefs I'm not just talkin' 'bout the team's, but the school's, the church's, and even your own daddy's interpretation of the scriptures. And we believe in your daddy, Ledyard. That's why we're here." He paused, saying with some discomfort, "I don't know when's the last time you opened your Bible, but Second Peter 2:1 through 2:2 says...."

"I know what Second Peter 2:1 through 2:2 says!" Ledyard sharply interjected.

"Maybe that was written for you," Roger said mildly.

"Yeah, and maybe it was written for my daddy," Ledyard countered less mildly.

Roger's mouth fell open in astonishment. "That's it, pal. Hope you have fun in hell!" Then he stalked off, stopping once to turn and add sarcastically, "I think ya had one too many out-of-body experiences, buddy. It's startin' to affect your brain!"

CLOUD DROPS

16

BULLY BENDER

> *But there were false prophets also among the people, even as there shall be false teachers among you....*
>
> *And many shall follow their pernicious ways....*
>
> *- II PETER 2:1 - 2:2*

"Yes?" Ledyard said, hurrying into the recreation room where his father and a young man who looked like a college linebacker were shooting a game of eightball.

About to take a shot, his father looked up. "Ah, Ledyard. There's someone I want you to meet." He returned to cuing-up his shot. When the reverend had seen Saturday morning's paper it hadn't taken him long to react. It was Tuesday evening and Ledyard was being introduced to his new chauffeur/bodyguard.

Ledyard glanced at the stranger with the lantern jaw and squared-off blond crewcut. The man caught his eye and smiled. It was not a warm smile but a rather oddly malicious one. And it immediately made Ledyard's blood run cold.

The reverend took his shot. The cue ball cracked off the eight ball and both slammed into corner pockets. "Durn!" he frowned, tossing his stick on the table, then looked up. "Come here, boy."

Ledyard joined them, the stranger laying his stick on the table as the reverend introduced him. "This is Billy Bender, your new chauffeur and guardian."

Even beneath the starched white shirt, tie, and sports coat Billy's bulging muscles were apparent. And at 6' 2" with a massive bull neck, even the 6' 1" reverend appeared small beside him. Above the previously broken nose were beady, ice-blue eyes. Twenty-seven-year-old Billy Bender smiled and extended his hand.

Ledyard warily took the dry, rough hand, but Billy slipped him a partial and squeezed the boy's fingers until Ledyard winced.

"Granger has been assigned to other duties. Mainly, servin' me. From now on Billy will be lookin' after your welfare." The reverend paused, frowning as he scrutinized Ledyard. "I trust you won't attempt to take advantage of Billy because he's new to our staff."

Ledyard avoided his father's eyes as he almost whispered, "No, sir."

"Good." The reverend straightened his tie and snugged his jacket before adding, "Then I'll leave you two to get acquainted." Without another word he left.

Embarrassed, taken completely by surprise, Ledyard didn't know where to look or what to say. Finally he looked at Billy, stuck his hand out and said with forced cheerfulness, "Hi, I'm Ledyard."

Billy looked at him deadpan. "We already did that."

"Oh. Yeah. I guess you're right," he shrugged. "Well, why don't you get the car out and we'll go to the gym and shoot some baskets?"

Billy Bender laughed heartily. *"You* don't tell *me* where we're goin' you spoiled little weirdo, I tell *you.* Got it?"

Ledyard stared at him in disbelief, then declared, "You're not talkin' to *me* like that!"

"Oh yeah?" Billy replied, taking a threatening step closer. "What're ya gonna do about it ya little pipsqueak?"

"What am I gonna do about it?" Ledyard laughed, "I'll show you what I'm gonna do about it!" He pivoted, about to storm from the room, but stopped in the doorway and turned. "Oh yeah, and y'all better start thinkin' about a new career move."

"We'll see about that!" Billy called after him as the boy turned and continued down the hall.

Ledyard found his father in his study tapping away at a word processor. He stopped in the doorway. "Daddy?"

Without looking up the reverend spoke while continuing to work the keyboard. "Make it short, boy, I'm preparin' next Sunday's sermon."

"Can I just have a minute? It's important."

Heaving an irritated sigh, the reverend looked up from the machine. "What?"

"It's about this new chauffeur, Billy Bender. He just called me a spoiled weirdo and refused to get the car when I asked. I want him fired immediately."

His father's burst of laughter was spontaneous. "Well you are a spoiled little weirdo, first of all, and second, who are you to be givin' orders to anybody? To tell you the truth that's why I hired him. To knock you off your high horse a might and teach you to respect your elders."

"But I'm 16 and don't need a...."

"And if he spoke rudely to you," his father went on, ignoring his son's protests, "well, all I can think is that you probably deserved it."

"But...."

"And furthermore, by a means that somehow escapes me you've grown into a 16-year-old smart aleck. You may have been able to manipulate Granger and take advantage of his good nature but you won't be able to do that with this man. I told him not to take any of your bull and I'm glad to hear he's taken me at my word. Now get out of here. I'm busy."

"But daddy!"

"Don't 'but daddy' me! You shouldn't have said that to those reporters and you know it. You did that deliberately."

"What? What did I say?" Ledyard demanded. "All I said was I didn't think God had anything to do with us winnin' the game!"

"Yes, practically at the same moment that I was on national television thankin' God for our successful season. It made a very nice story for the Chronicle, Ledyard, but your little ploy didn't go over well with me. I mean, every time I turn around you're contradictin' me or doin' somethin' to embarrass me! Now, the fact that you've chosen to compete with me rather than learn from me is your decision, but as long as that's the situation then I'll be doin' the hirin' and firin' around here. And as far as I'm concerned Billy Bender is a good Christian and an excellent disciplinarian. If you treat him with due respect instead of makin' demands and spoutin' orders then I'm sure y'all will get along just fine. So don't come whinin' to me about Billy Bender. That only tells me he's taken a firm hand with you and *that's* exactly what I want." The reverend turned back to tapping at his word processor.

"But...."

"That will be all, Ledyard," his father intoned without looking up from his work. "And shut the door on your way out."

With a sickening sense of despair Ledyard stepped out of the room and gently closed the door. Turning around, his face burned with embarrassment when he found Billy Bender standing there grinning like the Cheshire Cat, hands loosely clasped in front of him and rocking on the balls of his feet.

"I guess that settles that, doesn't it?" Billy said with a soft chuckle, adding, "now get dressed for the health club. I'm meeting some friends for a workout."

"But I just worked out an hour ago."

"Awww, you're breaking my heart."

At the health club built and maintained for staff, their families and any members of the congregation who wanted to join for an annual fee of $600 dollars, Ledyard slid down against the wall at the far end of the room and opened his book. There were only four guys in the free weights room.

Ledyard glanced over the top of his book as Billy came in. Billy located him, then joined the others in a workout with the barbells.

Turning the pages with unseeing eyes, Ledyard's mind was churning. He had to figure out a way of dealing with this guy. That Bender was a mental moron could end up being in Ledyard's favor though, he reasoned. In fact he might just end up with more freedom *now* than he'd ever had with the straitlaced and more sophisticated John Granger.

And then the thought struck. *He dislikes me as much as I dislike him.* Ledyard snapped his fingers. That part was good. Obviously anything but a straight shooter, Bender wanted his freedom as much as Ledyard wanted his own. If Ledyard played it real cool and drew him in until they became like coconspirators he could end up having more freedom than he'd ever dreamed of. Ledyard clapped the book closed, got to his feet and approached the bench where Bender was lifting.

Breathing heavily as he set the barbells in the cradle, Bender looked up at Ledyard and tersely asked, "What'd you want?"

"Would it be okay if I ran over to the library right quick to look somethin' up?"

Heaving a last deep breath, Bender sat up, eyeing him suspiciously. "I'm not supposed to let you out of my sight."

Ledyard shrugged. "I know, but when we get home, if I tell daddy I need to go there for school, you know he'll make you take me and then *you're* goin' to end up settin' around the library for a few hours. Maybe till closin' time."

Billy thought about this for a moment, scratching his jaw, then cocked his head, asking, "How long you gonna be gone?"

Ledyard shifted his feet and licked his lips, unsure of how much time to press for. "I'll be back in an hour."

Billy glanced at the wall clock, then leveled his gaze on Ledyard. "Okay," he warned, "but don't mess me up or I'll whip your hide up one side of the street and down the other."

"I won't," Ledyard quickly replied, "don't worry none about that."

"One hour," Billy said.

"Right. I'll be back here at 8:00 o'clock."

"Don't screw up, Ledyard."

"I won't."

Billy paused for an interminable moment, then said brusquely, "All right, get out of here."

"Thanks!" Ledyard grinned, "see ya at 8:00." He turned and quickly strode from the room.

Heart pounding with the anticipation of a whole hour of freedom, Ledyard crossed the lobby in quick strides and pushed through the glass doors. It was a balmy Texas evening in mid-October, the leave-rattling wind swaying the tall, mature trees that dotted the campus.

Drawing a deep breath of the musky, autumn-scented air, Ledyard had no destination in mind when he set off walking, he just wanted to breathe a free man and be alone with his thoughts. He laughed at the irony of it all. He'd almost been sick with despair at the prospect of life with Billy Bender. Several minutes later, though, he was facing an unanticipated *hour* of total freedom.

Ledyard suddenly realized he was walking towards the front gate and did a quick about-face. The last thing he wanted was to run into any guards. They would all recognize him immediately. He crossed the street, walked up a block and turned right at the corner.

Walking past the 5,000-seat auditorium, which also housed the television production facility, he spotted a handful of cars in the parking lot and wondered what went on there on Tuesday evenings. He had only been in the studio once or twice with his father. But that had been years ago when he was a little kid.

Except for around school, Ledyard was largely unknown to ministry staff and maintenance workers. The notoriety he had received the previous Friday had been unusual. By the tenth grade a lot of the other kids had caught up to him in size and stature and although an adequate player, he was no longer a star and consequently rarely even had his picture in the sports pages of the high school newspaper. This loss of star-status turned out to be a blessing in disguise, of course, even further reducing his profile on campus.

Ledyard left the sidewalk and walked across the damp grass for the rear of the building. Searching for an employee's entrance, he was already formulating a cock-and-bull story when he came around the corner and startled a young black man who quickly pivoted, dropped something and stepped on it. As he turned back, light from the mercury-vapor lamp over the door glinted off close-cropped kinky black hair.

Eyeing Ledyard rather harshly, he asked nervously, "Who're you?" But the indignant stare was really a bold cover of his own fear. Smoking was not allowed anywhere on campus. Even a janitor would not be hired without a signed vow giving up smoking as a condition of employment. The boy was hoping Ledyard hadn't seen the cigarette at all. Or smelled the smoke. But Ledyard had easily seen the glowing cigarette dropped in the dark. He also smelled it.

Well this is a fine start, Ledyard thought, quelling a smile. He loved it when it started out with him having something on the other guy instead of the other way around. He stuck his hand out and pleasantly inquired, "Who am I? I'm Ricky White, first semester freshman over at the college of communications. They told me there was a black dude workin' in the studio who would give me a glimpse of the production facility."

The kid put his hands on his hips and caught Ledyard's eye. "Now you ain't pullin' my leg, are you?"

"About what?"

"About being Ricky White," the boy replied. He thought he recognized Ledyard but couldn't place him.

Ledyard's brow furrowed momentarily as he thought, *Now who the heck is Ricky White?* He decided he would find out and looked up. Composed and pleasant-faced, he asserted, "Of course I'm Ricky White."

The boy burst out laughing and slapped his leg.

Cocking his head, Ledyard asked curiously, "Why? Who're you?"

Still grinning, the black kid shook his head. "You're not going to believe this."

"What?"

"*I'm* Ricky Brown!"

Ledyard almost fell on the ground laughing. "Now y'all ain't pullin' *my* leg, are you?" After the laughter subsided he asked, "Hey, ya ever get caught sneakin' a smoke before?" Ledyard wasn't about to let this kid get away without him knowing Ledyard had something on him.

Ricky Brown eyed Ledyard with furrowed brow. "No," he answered simply.

"I know ya h'ain't," Ledyard retorted, "because if ya had you wouldn't be workin' here right now. If they catch you breakin' your vow there's no second chance, it's just boom and they drop-kick you out of the program."

Ricky Brown was looking around, starting to get nervous. "Look, man," he said, shaking his head, "I really need this job. It's tough findin' one in this business. Especially right out of school."

Ledyard eyed him. "Well, one thing I've never been is a squealer, but now you owe me one."

"Oh, sure my man. No problem," Ricky Brown said, extending his hand and clasping Ledyard's briefly.

After a moment Ledyard said, "Well, Rick, did you want to show me the studio?"

Ricky Brown nodded, saying, "Sure, man, anytime except tonight."

"Why's that?" Ledyard frowned.

"'Cause I'm the only one working tonight and," he paused dramatically, "it's a top-secret project. Absolutely *nobody* without clearance is to be allowed in."

"Why?" Ledyard asked curiously. He could almost hear his father's voice in the way the boy had recited his orders. "What could a preacher possibly be doin' that would be so top-secret?"

Ricky Brown shook his head. He wasn't even going to discuss it. "Uh-uh, my man, no way. The first time I got to work this project they gave me a fat bonus. Same thing the second time. Well this is only my third time and I don't know what happened to the other dude I replaced, but I'm not risking it for you or anybody else. Like I said, come by *any* other time except Tuesday nights."

Ledyard fell silent, rolling a stone with the toe of his sneaker. After a moment he looked up and smiled pleasantly. "T'ain't good enough."

Ricky Brown nervously licked his lips. The kid had caught him red-handed. "You smoke?" he asked.

Ledyard grinned and winked. "I do everything."

Feeling a little more sure, Ricky decided it was better to risk possible trouble in lieu of the guaranteed job-loss he was facing if the kid squealed. Eyeing Ledyard carefully, he asked in a low, quick voice, "Like pictures of neckid women?"

Ledyard shrugged. "I don't know. Never seen a neckid women before." He leaned closer, elbowing his new friend in the ribs and saying with a grin, "But it does sound right interestin'!" Even as he was speaking, though, he was thinking, *naked women!*

"Well, all right," Ricky was saying, "but you gotta promise not to breathe a word of this to anyone."

Ledyard held up a hand. "Promise."

"Okay, my man, I'm trustin' ya."

"You won't regret it," Ledyard answered evenly.

Ricky glanced at his watch. "Holy smokes! He'll be callin' for tape any minute!"

"How many people know about this?" Ledyard asked as Ricky hurriedly turned for the door.

"Just the reverend and eleven other men so far. And me of course, the tape operator."

Ledyard followed him in, Ricky holding onto the door and gently easing it closed. They were backstage, the area dimly lit with a single red bulb. Ledyard could hear the echo of his father's disembodied voice in the massive, largely deserted auditorium. "...And what you will witness tonight, gentlemen, is just the latest Hollywood-generated porno filth that is spreadin' throughout our society, poisonin' the minds and futures of America's youth...."

In the dimness were narrow steps leading upwards. "This is back of the stage," Ricky whispered, gesturing towards the stairs. "Control room is up there."

"And if we're ever goin' to put a stop to it...."

Ledyard could hear his father carrying on as he mounted the steps.

"...We've got to be familiar with just what it is we're fightin'. In short, gentlemen, know thine enemy!"

Ricky Brown, 22, recent college graduate and production assistant for Christian Condensed Television (CCTV), spoke over his shoulder as he led Ledyard through the TV control room and gestured at a bank of monitors. "This is where the director sits and calls the shots. Each camera is connected to one of these monitors so the director can see exactly what the camera sees."

Beneath the monitors was a long, narrow strip of one-way window. By leaning across the counter Ledyard could gaze out upon the vastness of the vacant auditorium and the stage far below. From up there his father appeared very small, as did the huddle of 11 men in the first row center listening with rapt attention. Ledyard thought he recognized several of the men: his father's business manager, Harry Wigglesworth; the principal of his high school, Mr. Winthrop; Mr. Thorton, his Bible class teacher; and John Granger. The others were from the board of elders. Men he had only met formally years ago and didn't really know.

His father's voice was even louder in the control room, coming directly through the system's speakers. "...As y'all will shortly witness for yourselves, gentlemen, the material is designed solely to shock and titillate, without a single redeeming social value or feature...."

Ricky leaned across the counter and pointed out the window. "That's the man himself talkin' on stage right now."

"I know," Ledyard softly replied, "I seen him on television before."

"Oh." Without further comment Ricky moved to the Grass Valley Switcher with its vast array of buttons, fader bars, lights and meters. "This is where the technical director sits and controls what goes out over the air," he explained. "The director calls out what he wants over this speaker/headphone system," he picked up the headset lying on the counter, "and the TD punches up whatever camera or special effect the director calls for."

"Wow!" Ledyard exclaimed as he scanned the control panel. "You'd have to be a pilot to fly one of these things!"

Ricky laughed. "Oh, it's not really as difficult as it looks."

He continued through a doorway to the next room. It also had a series of monitors, along with a bank of six video recorders and various exotic-looking oscilloscopes, instruments and knobs for synchronizing the cameras, adjusting color and brightness levels and checking signal strength.

"This is tape control," Ricky continued, "the person at this station is responsible for getting the tapes rolling, having taped segments cued-up, things like that."

"It all looks right complicated," Ledyard was saying when Ricky suddenly held up a hand for silence.

The reverend's voice came loudly into the room, "Okay, let's get the screen up, dim the lights and roll tape."

"That's me," Ricky said, rushing back into the control room. He stopped at the switcher and punched two buttons, then leaned over and looked out the long narrow window.

From the center of the stage a large-screen TV rose out of the floor and locked in place.

"You're not going to believe this," Ricky said, hurrying past Ledyard as he returned to tape control and punched a button on the panel. Instantly several of the monitor screens in both rooms lit up as the tape rolled through its five-second countdown. He quickly turned to a bank of dimmer switches and lowered the houselights to an orangish glow.

On the monitors titles were rolling over a background of a car making its way through city streets, cheap canned music for a soundtrack.

Turning from the dimmer switches, Ricky glanced up at the bank of monitors to make sure everything looked right, then seized one of three thickly upholstered castor-wheeled chairs and shoved it at Ledyard. "Here, have a seat," he said, plopping into another chair and leaning back to gaze up at the glowing screens. "Our work's done for the time being."

Ledyard pulled the chair around and sat down. On the screen was a shot of a postman carrying his mailbag as he strode jauntily from house to house posting letters. The next shot was inside a house. A living room. A young woman peeked between closed drapes to view the mailman coming up the sidewalk. She let the drapes go, turned towards the camera and pulled her dress off over her head.

Ledyard couldn't believe his eyes. She was stark naked, her firm, upturned breasts quivering and her dark muff looming huge as she walked at the camera and past to give the viewer a look at her shapely tush.

Getting up, Ledyard went into the control room and peered through the long, narrow window. Against the background of the immense, royal-blue carpeting, the orange glow of the dimmed lights on their shiny, excited faces, the church elders, teachers, and administrators looked like cartoon caricatures of demons in hell cackling with devious delight.

When Ledyard returned to tape control, dropped into his chair and looked up at the screen, the postman was in the house now and slowly undressing.

Staring, mouth agape, Ledyard couldn't believe it. After all the ranting his father did over pornography, and now he sat grinning with his cronies, obviously enjoying the show, and all under the flimsy guise of learning what not to watch! Ledyard couldn't help thinking what gross hypocrites they all were. He shifted uncomfortably in his chair as the moaning and groaning began. In his entire life he had never seen a naked woman before, let alone a couple copulating on a living room floor.

Over the years, though, he had gone out with quite a few girls. But after three or four dates, the ever present watchdog Granger supervising, the girls all reacted the same way—with a sympathetic grimace when they said goodbye. And then he never saw them again. Or at least never socialized with them again. As if he had leprosy or something the way they suddenly and studiously avoided him in the halls at school.

Word got around. Going out with Ledyard was like having a boyfriend in prison. There were only certain visiting hours, and then under the watchful gaze of the guards. The superstar preacher couldn't have his son getting caught in any compromising situations. After all, the boy was unstable and might get taken advantage of by an unscrupulous girl. After awhile Ledyard gave up asking girls out. It got embarrassing always being turned down.

"Oooh wheee!" A grinning Ricky glanced back over his shoulder, "What'a you think of this?"

Ledyard forced a smile. "Great family entertainment."

Ricky turned back to the screen, saying, "Now you know why it's top-secret!"

Ledyard had to chuckle. "No doubt."

When the show was over Ricky turned the houselights up, lowered the screen, and popped the tape out of the machine. "I'll be right back," he said. "Wait here and don't touch anything."

"Where're you goin'?"

"To deliver this tape to the rev," Ricky answered, holding up the cassette. "He always takes these with him personally when he leaves. Be right back." Ricky bounded out the door and down the metal stairs, the thumping of his feet rapidly receding.

Ledyard got up and returned to the control room, once again peering through the strip of one-way window. A moment later he saw Ricky walk onto the stage and hand his father the tape, then noticed something pressed into Ricky's hand. Probably his "bonus."

He sat down in one of the large, upholstered swivel chairs and leaned back, putting his feet up on the counter and crossing them at the ankles. It had been two years since his out-of-body experience. In the meantime he had received a few messages, but that was about it. For the life of him he couldn't figure out why the Invisible Ones came and went as they did. Well, it was about time for them to come back again. And he was anxiously awaiting their return. If he got out of his body again, this time he wasn't going back—ever.

Ledyard suddenly sat up, heart pounding. Shoes thumping against metal stairs were coming straight at him. A moment later he almost sighed with relief as Ricky turned into the room and loudly proclaimed, "Hey, buddy!" He grinned and held out his hand, "We got away with it. They're gone."

Ledyard smiled, bounced out of the chair and slapped him five. "I knew you could do it!" He glanced at his watch: 7:50. Ten minutes to get back to the health club. He grabbed Ricky's hand, "Well, gotta be goin', Mr. Brown. Homework."

Ricky laughed and said, "Well, okay, Mr. White. Come around anytime. You know where I'm at."

"Will-Co Roger and out!" Ledyard said with a grin and headed for the exit. In the doorway he stopped and turned, catching Ricky's eye. "I'll be back, man."

Ricky nodded and winked. "I'll be lookin' forward to it, my man."

It only took five minutes to get back to the health club. Billy Bender, gym bag in hand, was pacing the lobby floor. "You're lucky you got back in time," he said as Ledyard pulled the glass door open and came in.

"I'm early," Ledyard pointed out, adding, "I'm a man of my word."

"Good. Let's go."

The stretch limo was in a no parking zone in the circular drive, Billy Bender going around to the driver's side as Ledyard got in back. This chauffeur wasn't about to open doors for some punk kid. At least not when the reverend, who was very appearance-conscious, wasn't around.

CLOUD DROPS

17

GOD AND THE AMERICAN ECONOMY

> *The father shall be divided against the son,*
> *and the son against the father....*
> *- LUKE 12:53*

The Reverend Pat Patterson didn't attend his son's sporting events. He was just too recognizable. In the past it had always ended in a melee of adoring fans pressing in from all sides, sometimes keeping him trapped for hours signing autographs or asking embarrassing questions he was unprepared to answer. And bringing enough body-guards to surround him while they pushed through the crowd so he could escape in his limousine made a very bad impression on the simple folk who were his most ardent fans. In the end it was just bad PR and always had been, so he avoided the situation altogether.

Now he had another PR problem that would not so eas-ily be resolved. Ledyard. He heard the front door open and tossed Ledyard's neatly typed Bible class assignment on his desk. In four quick strides he crossed to the door of the den, opened it and stuck his head out.

Ledyard was just coming down the hall. "Would you come in here a moment?" his father asked rather sharply and threw the door aside.

Ledyard stepped into the den and stopped uneasily just inside the door.

Snatching the paper up, the reverend turned and sat on the corner of his desk, one foot on the floor. "Shut the door and come here, boy," he ordered.

Ledyard closed the door and turned around. "Sit down," his father said, gesturing to one of two thickly upholstered leather chairs before his immense mahogany desk. Warily eyeing his father, Ledyard crossed to the farthest chair and sank into it.

"Do you know what this is?" he asked, holding up the three-page Bible class assignment by the stapled corner like it was a putrid, odorous thing.

"No," Ledyard shook his head. "All I can see is the back."

"This," his father intoned ominously, "is the paper on God and the American Economy that you turned in for Mr. Thorton's Bible class. He was so disturbed by it that he came to see me this evenin'."

Ledyard winced, stammering, "W-What's so disturbin' about it?"

"What's so disturbin' about it?" his father mimicked, nodding slightly. "Well, let's see." His eyes narrowed as he examined the first page. "Oh. Okay. First page, second paragraph; I quote: *That a substantial number of Americans are homeless, trapped in cruel cycles of poverty that relegates them to livin' in ghettos, unemployed or otherwise unable to make a wage that meets the cost of livin' is not evidence of an individual's lack of faith or belief in God. Rather, it is evidence of an imperfect system that is not always able to provide enough jobs for the available number of workers."*

Here the reverend paused, raising his voice to an uncomfortable volume as he continued reading; *"To suggest that unemployment and the resultant poverty is an act of God visited upon unbelievers is, in fact, to ascribe to God responsibility for man's failure to come up with a more effective means of distributing the necessities of life. As scripture teaches, to ascribe to God acts which are done by men is to blaspheme the Holy Spirit—the one offense that, according to Jesus, will not be forgiven."*

Holding his son with a hard stare, the reverend slowly lowered the paper. "Do you realize what you're sayin'?"

Ledyard nodded dully.

"This sorry piece of trash you've written is an indictment of *everything* I teach!" He tossed the paper on his desk and stood up. "Do you even know what I teach? Do you listen?"

Again Ledyard nodded dully, eyes unfocused, staring off at some distant point in space.

"I teach what is commonly referred to as *wealth theology.* An understandin' of God's word that I have achieved through years of study and now am attemptin' to pass on to others. And the fact that *we* are wealthy is evidence of the success of the very thing I teach. Do you understand that?"

Ledyard locked eyes with his father. "So poverty is evidence of a person's lack of faith, and wealth evidence of strong faith?"

"Exactly! And not just evidence of faith, but evidence of livin' right by the word of God! He don't want *his* people livin' in poverty! Jesus said, and I quote, *I am come that they might have life, and that they might have it more abundantly*—John 10:10!"

Leaping to his feet, Ledyard shouted, "Throughout scripture Jesus rails *against* materialism! In John 10:10 Jesus is clearly talkin' about eternal *life,* NOT material wealth! How can you so totally screw up this simple teachin'? Because you *want* to. Because by corruptin' scripture and pervertin' the simple truths of Jesus you're able to buffalo your followers into sendin' you money! But in deceivin' them you've also deluded yourself into believin' you're somehow servin' God when all you're really servin' is your own stone-cold heart and the lusts of your flesh!" Fixing his father with an angry stare, winded, heart pounding, Ledyard dropped into the big leather chair.

Exploding with rage, the Reverend Pat Patterson grabbed his son by the shirtfront and yanked him to his feet, their faces inches apart. "Look, you smart ass!" he shrieked, Ledyard blinking against a rain of spittle getting in his eyes, nose and mouth, "you know a better preacher or a better church than the one I've built!?" Shoving him with a force that sent the boy stumbling backwards where he fell over the chair and hit the floor with a reverberating *boom!*, the preacher bellowed, "Then go there!" Blowing like a beached whale, his face red, he snatched the paper off his desk and threw it at his son. "Now get the hell out of here!"

Stunned, Ledyard grabbed his report, leaped to his feet and bolted for the door. Throwing it open and dashing out, he collided with his mother who had been outside listening and hadn't retreated fast enough. He caught her by the elbows to keep them both from falling.

Mumbling an apology, he glanced at her and was shocked by the hard look on her face.

Brusquely jerking free of him, she ordered, "Go to your room!"

After he was gone she turned into the den and softly closed the door. Her husband was sitting slumped behind his desk. As she sank into one of the chairs he looked up. Almost trembling, he said, "We've got to do somethin' about that boy."

"Well I don't know what," she sighed. "I wonder why Doral Doberts doesn't have this problem with *his* son?" She paused, then continued half seriously, "Maybe we should call down to Doral Doberts University and ask his advice."

"Doral Doberts!" Her husband spat the words. He'd lost all respect for the man after the Tulsa, Oklahoma preacher went on TV and told his followers to send millions or God was going to kill him. After a moment's contemplation the Texas preacher leaned back and put a hand to his forehead with a weary sigh. "Maybe we should send Ledyard to live with your parents in Florida."

"Oh sure," his wife said caustically. "We'd have a lot of control over him there. Why, just this mornin' I had a reporter call from the *Observer.* That's an East Coast paper, by the way. Wanted to speak to Ledyard. When I asked what about he said he wanted to know if it was true that Ledyard didn't believe in prayer!"

"So what'd you do?"

"I told him of *course* Ledyard believes in prayer. Then I hung up on him."

"Good."

"Anyway, that's all we need, to have him livin' in Florida with my folks. Why, as soon as the press found out, and you know they would, probably within hours, he'd be spoutin' off his insane ideas to every...."

"Wait!" her husband cried, suddenly sitting up. "That's it!"

"What's it?" Brenda May frowned.

"You just said it, Brenda May. That boy is *insane!*" He sniffed, adding after a moment, "Or at least mentally disturbed, anyway."

Leaning forward in her chair, she whispered, "Are you sayin' we should have him committed?"

He shrugged. "Why not? We'll put him in one of those nice private places. Tell them about Ledyard's experiences with invisible people, hearin' voices and what not. Then, when the psychiatrists start questioning him and hear it for themselves they'll start a treatment program."

"And?" Brenda May questioned.

"And once Ledyard starts hearin' how goofy his ideas are from someone else besides *us,* well, it'll be an objective disinterested third party, and maybe that fact alone will wake him up to how off the wall he's been acting lately."

Brenda May Patterson leaned back in her chair and smiled. "You know, sometimes I think you're a genius!"

"And what's more," her husband went on excitedly, "anything further that Ledyard does manage to get into the press will certainly have less credence comin' from someone institutionalized on a mental ward."

"You're right," his wife said briskly. "There must be several nice institutions in the Houston area."

"Good. Look into it first thing tomorrow, but," he cautioned, "don't let them know who you are or what any of this is about. We certainly wouldn't want this comin' out before Ledyard goes in."

"No, of course not," his wife agreed. "First we'll have to do a little research, settle on the right place, have all the arrangements made and then make our move swiftly before anyone, most of all Ledyard, even knows what's goin' on."

"Precisely," the reverend smiled and flipped his pencil into the air.

CLOUD DROPS

18

VISITATION

> *Jesus saith unto her, Touch me not; for I am*
> *not yet ascended to my Father....*
> *- John 20:17*

Ledyard looked down at the paper in his hand as he turned into his bedroom and shut the door. Who had actually graded it with a large red "F" he wondered, Mr. Thorton or his father? Ah, who cared anyway? He tossed the paper on his desk.

Being the son of a minister who frequently ranted about the evils of rock and roll, that particular type of music had not been a part of Ledyard's life. In fact it had been banned from the campus since the founding of the ministry. Lately though, Ledyard had taken to tuning in a local rock station out of Houston and with the volume low, secretly listening late at night. And the more he heard the more he was baffled by his father's narrow-minded attitude. The whole spectrum of rock music was such a kaleidoscope of sound, images, energy and emotion! How could anyone pronounce *all* of it, in one fell swoop, the devil's music?

Tuning in the station now, he kicked off his sneakers, dropped onto his bed, tucked his hands behind his head and lay staring at the ceiling, the music low, someone singing that every day was judgment day. Ledyard agreed with that sentiment, but God help him if he should express it to his father. Wondering how much more he could take he dozed off praying, as he often had over the last two years, for his Invisible Friends to come and get him the heck out again. Hopefully permanently.

It was some kind of weird techno-music, the singer telling everyone to elevate from the norm, the music gently prodding Ledyard's subconscious. He'd never heard the song before, but it struck a chord in him and he opened his eyes. And shut his eyes. And then opened them again and jerked upright in bed.

Holy smokes! What was it? He opened his mouth to shout for his father but the thought that it might go away stopped him. He tore his eyes away to glance at the glowing red numerals of the digital clock on his nightstand. Two a.m.

Instantly his eyes reverted back to... *what was it?* An amazing wheel of fire, or some kind of laser-light, the most beautiful blue color he'd ever laid eyes on.

Slowly revolving, it gradually moved closer to the foot of his bed. There it hovered turning this way and that, inverting itself, rotating like a gyro, tiny nips of blue flame flaring off the edges. It leveled out again for a good 30 seconds before raising up seemingly to gaze at him.

Then to his utter astonishment words actually began to come from the wheel, but Ledyard was so awe-struck he heard not a single one. Even if he had thought of reaching out to touch it, to see if it was real, he couldn't have moved just then to save his life.

Struggling to focus his ears to just what it was saying, his mind reeling, he suddenly understood. It was saying his name... *without making any sound!*

"L-Lord?" Ledyard stammered, trembling so hard the bed shook.

"It's not the Lord, Ledyard," the flaming wheel said evenly.

"Sorry," Ledyard managed to croak through a throat tight with fear. And then he seemed to hear laughter coming from the wheel.

"There is only one King of Kings," the wheel continued, "we reserve 'Lord' for Him."

"Okay," Ledyard acknowledged shakily. After a moment's silence, the subtle, steady hissing of the flaming wheel the only sound, he took a deep breath. Struggling to control his trembling voice, he asked, "Wha... who... are *you,* then?"

Again soft laughter from the wheel. "A servant of the Lord, Ledyard."

"You are?" Ledyard was still beside himself and by no means used to talking to a brilliant blue laser-wheel of burning light hovering in the darkness at the foot of his bed.

The wheel almost seemed to nod. No—by God it *did* nod its reply!

"You can nod, too?" Ledyard asked in amazement.

"Can't you?" the wheel pleasantly replied.

Ledyard nodded, grinning so hard it almost hurt. "I love the way you talk."

"That's funny," the wheel replied, "we love the way you *act.*"

"You do?" Ledyard asked, his voice rising.

"Yes. When you were a little tyke you were so unafraid of anything. I'll never forget the first time we met out by the walnut tree in your backyard."

Startled, Ledyard exclaimed, "It's y'all! I thought I recognized the voice!"

The wheel laughed delightedly, "Yes, it's me."

"I always forget to ask your name."

"Cambian."

"Yes, that's it. I remember now. Y'all told me the first time we met. God, that seems like such a long time ago!"

"Yet it seems just like yesterday, too."

"Where're your friends?" Ledyard asked.

"Waiting for me on a cloud drifting somewhere east of here," Cambian answered.

Grinning, Ledyard nodded. After a moment he said, "Funny, earlier tonight I was prayin' for y'all to come back and rescue me."

For some moments the flaring wheel dimmed, silently turning round and round in its slow, calm way. Finally Ledyard inquired, "It was y'all who came and pulled me out of my body a couple of years ago, wasn't it?"

"Yes."

"And then y'all went off and left me," Ledyard said, revealing a trace of hurt. "I would've come with you."

"That's why we took off," the wheel softly replied. "It's not time for you to come with us. We just wanted to give you a sense of the reality of the life that's all around you. To get you ready for the long haul."

Ledyard leaned back on one elbow, asking with disappointment, "Then I can't come with y'all tonight?"

"No, Ledyard. We need you here."

"But why? I would *die* for the Lord!" Ledyard declared, sitting up again.

The creature of fire and light chuckled softly before answering, "Dying for the Lord's the easy part, Ledyard, it's *living* for the Lord that's difficult. But one day you will come with us," he continued, "I promise. First, though, you've got to complete your mission here."

"But what *is* my mission here?" Ledyard anxiously asked.

The wheel flared for a moment before softly explaining, "What we have here on Earth right now is a case of a broad mass of people who have evolved into worshipping their religion, the creature, instead of God, the Creator."

Ledyard nodded thoughtfully. "Yeah, I know what you mean there. You're talkin' about Romans 1:25."

"Right. And we were hoping that we could get you to put forth our views," the wheel continued, "and you have."

"Yeah, well, t'ain't done much good, has it?" Ledyard intoned. "What y'all need is to get my daddy on your side. He's the preacher and he believes, let me tell you!"

"That's what worries us. The fact that he believes and yet is so totally deceived. You see, your father has a lot of power, wealth and fame, and he achieved that through corrupting the word of God and misleading the people. Now the Lord feels it will take *more* than a miracle to get him to turn his back on all of that, which is exactly what we would be asking him to do. And more, actually. For it would require him to reverse himself on so many things he holds dear—like Wealth Theology for example. We're afraid he might find it easier to die in a lie than to live in the truth. That's why we started coming to you when you were just a small boy. To get to you before *they* got to you, and then see how you would carry the truth we gave you. Now we have no doubt."

"But what am *I* supposed to do?"

"Keep pushing for the truth. Convince your father."

Ledyard heaved a sigh and shook his head. "I've been tryin', but as y'all probably already know, I haven't gotten too far." He paused. "Did y'all see his reaction to my Bible class report?"

"No."

"Well it's goin' to take more than me talkin' to him, I can guarantee y'all that. But if *you* appeared before him...."

"That's exactly how I feel, Ledyard," the wheel continued, "and when I return I'm going to argue in favor of just such a miracle. You see, we only get one shot at this. I'm going to take on a body of flesh and blood. A permanent appearance, so to speak, and I'm going to argue for making that appearance before your father."

Suddenly sitting up straighter, Ledyard exclaimed, "That would be great! That would work! I just know it would! How could he deny somethin' like that happenin' before his very own eyes?"

"That's exactly what I'm going to argue before the Lord," Cambian quietly said, his words coming from the fiery wheel. "But I can't make any promises, Ledyard, because it's not up to me. Do you understand?"

Ledyard nodded, "I know." Distracted by another thought, he grinned, asking, "Can I touch you?"

Cambian chuckled. "No. I'm electromagnetic energy and running very hot tonight so you can easily see and hear me, and I wouldn't want to burn you." After a moment he seemed to smile and say, "Bye, Ledyard."

Ledyard grinned, making an upward gesture with his head. "Bye, Cambian."

"Well, I guess I'll be off then," Cambian said, the wheel seeming to speed up with a steadily growing rushing sound. It flared and flattened out. "Keep up the good work!"

"Wait!" Ledyard cried, "when will y'all be back?"

The voice came at a higher pitch as the wheel accelerated, growing ever brighter till Ledyard began shielding his eyes. "Whenever the Lord sends me…" it answered, the sound of Cambian's voice fading into an indecipherable high-pitched whine. Then the wheel turned up on its axis and sped through the closed window without shattering the glass or so much as ruffling the curtains.

For a second Ledyard sat there staring, mouth agape. Then he tossed the blankets aside, leapt from his bed, ran to the window and peered out at the sky. It was a clear, moonless night. He frowned. There was no sign of the fiery wheel arcing across the sky as he had expected. All he could see were stars. Billions of them. Twinkling diamonds stretching off across the black velvet of the eternal universe in every direction.

With a sigh he returned to his bed and fell face-down, exhausted, the tension draining from him like water running off a roof. Then he drifted into a deep and dreamless sleep.

CLOUD DROPS

19

ORDINARY MAN

> *...blessed are they that have not seen, and yet have believed.*
> *- JOHN 20:29*

When Ledyard opened his eyes the next morning he was surprised. Sitting up, he explored his surroundings. Everything seemed so normal but everything was so different. Or was it his perspective that had changed? On the stereo a band he'd never heard before was singing about leading the sheep from the slaughter.

He turned and stared at the machine. Reaching for the remote control on the nightstand, he tapped the OFF button and sat up straighter, bracing himself with the heels of his hands. He'd had dreams before. At his age, though, they usually involved some girl he fancied and were so vivid and lifelike that he woke up hoping she wasn't downstairs in the nude talking to his parents. But last night had been no dream. The memory of it was much too real. The conversation....

And they were going to do a miracle. Yawning, he reached for a knuckle-cracking stretch, threw off the covers and jumped out of bed. He had to tell someone. Predicting the miracle would prove he wasn't crazy. That he'd been telling the truth all along.

Having fallen asleep in his clothes, he changed into jeans and a gray sweatshirt and sat on the edge of the bed near the nightstand, put his sneakers on and reached for the phone. Dialing Roger's number, he tucked the phone in his shoulder and turned to tying the laces. "Hello, Roger? Ledyard. I've got to talk to you. Somethin' happened last night. No, just meet me at the football field. Yes, I'm leavin' as soon as I hang up. Okay, bye."

Ledyard clicked off the phone, set it down, grabbed his blue windbreaker from the closet and left, bounding down the grand staircase and out the front door. Screw Billy Bender and his parents he thought as he set a quick pace down the bricked circular drive and out the front gate. Since today was reserved for parent-teacher conferences there were no classes.

At the football field at the top of the bleachers he spotted Roger leaning casually against the rail. Racing up the concrete steps two at a time, Ledyard arrived sweaty and winded and talking excitedly. "He came last night, Roger! I actually *saw* him, and you wouldn't believe it! They're gonna do a miracle!"

"Whoa! Whoa!" Roger exclaimed, "slow down and catch your breath before you die of a heart attack!"

Ledyard doubled over and came up sucking a huge breath of air, then wiped at his sweaty forehead with a sleeve. After his breathing stabilized he started again. "Okay, I know over the last few years y'all started thinkin' maybe I been losin' my cattle. To tell you the truth sometimes I've wondered myself." He paused, eyeing his friend.

"Yes?" Roger invited him to continue.

"But last night they came back again. Or at least one of them did. Only this time I *saw* him, Roger, with my own two eyes. And *spoke* with him face to face!"

"Are you tellin' me that a man appeared out of thin air right before your eyes?" Roger frowned.

"Yes!" Ledyard exclaimed. "I mean no. I mean, yes, but he didn't look like no ordinary man."

"You sound confused," Roger carefully replied, watching him closely. "Are you sure it weren't no dream?"

"No!" Ledyard almost shouted, "it really happened. But you'd never believe what he looked like unless you saw it yourself!"

"I don't know," Roger said warily. "You still sound confused to me." He paused, "The question is, what did he look like? A right simple question I'd say. You got a problem with that?"

"No, Roger," Ledyard shook his head. "I just wonder if you'll believe me."

"You said a man appeared out of thin air," Roger impatiently reiterated. "And all I said was, 'what'd he look like?'"

Self-consciously shifting from one foot to the other, Ledyard blurted, "Well, he was... they... that is, *we* take on a different form when we die. I mean, if y'all believe in life after death then you must believe we take on some sort of form after death."

"No," Roger flatly replied. "When you die your soul goes to be with Jesus."

"Exactly!" Ledyard cried. "And what does that soul look like?"

"It don't look like nothin', Ledyard, it's just your spirit, and it's invisible."

"I thought you didn't believe in invisible people?" Ledyard countered.

"I don't!" Roger shot back. "I didn't say *people* are invisible, I said your *soul* is invisible."

"Roger," Ledyard intoned, "the simple fact is that if you believe in eternal life and a judgment day and all of that then you must believe that we somehow survive as identifiable personalities."

"Okay," Roger grudgingly admitted. "So what?"

"So what do you suppose this identifiable personality looks like after the meat of its body is gettin' ate by worms?"

"Okay, Ledyard, tell me, but you sure talk weird," Roger informed him, putting hands on hips.

"Okay," Ledyard calmly began, "I'll tell ya. When you die, what survives is your aural-electrical field. And your memories, personality, thoughts, everything is held in what *they* call your electromagnetic body. Now, when I saw this person last night he was in the form of this, like, energy field in the shape of a wheel about this big," he held his hands up some three feet apart. "And it was, like, *burnin'*, but this guy, Cambian's his name, said they only look like that when they travel. Otherwise they simply generate bodies of a sort when they're walkin' around under gravity."

Roger was looking at his friend gravely. After a moment he said, "Why're you tellin' me all this, Ledyard? Are you tryin' to make yourself out to be some sort of holy man or twenty-first century prophet or what?" Suddenly he scoffed loudly, "Oh, all hail Ledyard! Ledyard the Messiah has returned! All hail the great Ledyard Patterson, prophet of God who holds the secret to eternal life!" He laughed in his face, saying, "No thanks, Ledyard. I ain't buyin' it." Shaking his head, he turned and started down the cement stairs.

"Wait, Roger, there's one thing you should know," Ledyard called after him.

Roger stopped and turned. "Yeah? What?"

Seeing the scorn on his face, Ledyard sighed. "Forget it."

"I don't want to know," Roger sneered, then turned and continued down the stairs.

Ledyard stood at the rail until Roger was a tiny forlorn figure plodding across the turf beneath a cold gray sky threatening rain. Somehow things weren't working out the way he'd planned. Oh well. What had he expected? Even if Roger had tried to believe him, Ledyard couldn't hold it against him for not because he couldn't imagine *himself* believing such a tale if Roger had brought it to him.

He felt a single raindrop hit one side of his face as he started down the bleacher steps. It rolled down his cheek like a tear. Wondering what to do next the idea flashed through his mind so clearly he couldn't believe he hadn't thought of it before. He was going to phone Ricky Brown. Videotape. That would work.

In the foyer of the library he stopped at the pay phone, looked up the TV production facility in the campus phone book, dug out a quarter, fed it to the machine and dialed. After a moment he spoke into the receiver. "Yes, is Ricky Brown there?" He nodded, "Tell him Ricky White is calling. I think he'll want to talk to me. Oh, okay then, I'll just meet him at the backdoor."

Ricky Brown wasn't feeling good as he left the studio and went down to the rear door to meet Ledyard. He had figured out who Ricky White was. And that made him nervous.

He pushed the door open and looked outside just as Ledyard came around the corner of the building. Pushing the door wide, he backed up as Ledyard ducked in out of the rain, then let the door slam shut. Eyeing one another in the dim crimson light backstage of the darkened auditorium,

Ricky said evenly, "I know who you are. I saw you at the football game."

Ledyard shrugged. "I know."

"Well what you want with me, man?" Ricky asked suspiciously.

"I want to make a very short tape. To talk about somethin' that happened to me. Then later I'll have proof."

"Proof of what?"

"Proof that I knew..." Here Ledyard faltered, unsure of how to continue, then looked the kid in the eye and asked bluntly, "Do you believe in God?"

With a dry little cough Ricky glanced down momentarily, sniffed, looked at Ledyard and asked, "Don't everybody?"

Ledyard stared at him. "Ah, I know what it is," he said after a moment. "You believe in God, you just don't believe in my daddy."

Ricky jerked imperceptibly. "Y-Yeah," he stammered in surprise, "you're right."

"Well neither do I."

Ricky looked up, astonished. "You don't!?" he exclaimed.

"No. Now tell me the truth, do you believe in the supernatural—in God?"

"If I didn't why would I lie about it?" Ricky asked emphatically. "If I was goin' to lie about anything I would've lied about not believin' in your daddy."

Ledyard nodded. "Yeah, I guess that makes sense." After a thoughtful moment he asked, "Would you believe me if I told you I've been havin' experiences with the supernatural since I was six years old?"

Ricky shrugged. "What sort of supernatural experiences?"

"Experiences like bein' contacted by men. Men who were here on Earth before but who are now in their supernatural state."

"You mean ghosts," Ricky said flatly.

"If you want to put it that way," Ledyard replied, "but they don't look like ghosts. And they can travel across the universe because they have no time or space limitations."

Ricky shook his head. "I don't understand. How can they have no time or space limitations?"

"To tell you the truth I don't rightly understand it either. But I've been talkin' to them telepathically for years and last night for the first time I actually *saw* one of these guys. I swear to God it's the truth!"

"Why you?" Ricky asked.

Ledyard shrugged, "Why not?"

"And I suppose they have some message they want you to get out?"

"Naturally."

"Which is?"

"Well, it's a lot of things really. They're not happy with the job the present preachers are doin' for one thing."

"Including your daddy's preaching?"

"Absolutely."

Ricky frowned and rubbed his forehead, then caught Ledyard's eye. "Can I ask you something?"

"Sure."

"How do you know you're not just like, imagining these things? Or dreamin' them at night and wakin' up in the mornin' thinkin' they actually happened? You know, I've had dreams before that were so real...."

"Wait a minute," Ledyard held up a hand. "I've had dreams before too. And that's exactly how I know my experiences with these whatever-you-want-to-call-them people were real. I can tell the difference between dreams and reality. Can't you? But," he hastened to add, "I don't really care if you believe me or not. I don't expect it and it's not important. What is important is that you help me."

"Help you what?"

"Make a short videotape. Last night they told me they were maybe goin' to do a miracle soon for the benefit of my daddy. They called it 'appearance in the flesh.' What I want to do is describe some of my experiences on tape. Then, if they do this thing, whatever it is, I'll have proof that I knew all along. I want to prove to my daddy that I've been tellin' him the truth. It's important that he believe me if for no other reason than his own salvation. And that's no joke. We're talkin' about life and death here."

Ricky thought about it a moment, then slowly nodded. "I see. Well, that sounds reasonable enough, my man." He glanced at his watch. "A crew is supposed to come in at 1:00 o'clock to tape some short promos. It's 10:00 now. That gives us three hours. Think that's enough time?"

Ledyard grinned, "More than enough."

"Okay, let's get started."

Upstairs in the studio Ricky explained the procedure as he moved about snapping on switches and adjusting controls. When everything was ready he pointed at a monitor. "See, camera three is aimed right at stage center where the podium is. You just stand there, hold up the newspaper for a minute or so as proof of the date, and start talking when I give the word over the public address."

"But the date is so tiny they'll never be able to see it on TV," Ledyard protested.

"Don't matter, my man," Ricky answered. "All they got to make out is the headline."

"Right," Ledyard said, picking up the folded *Houston Chronicle* Ricky had brought that morning. Pausing at the door, he added, "Thanks."

"No problem," Ricky smiled. As soon as Ledyard was gone he got up and went to tape control, loaded a cassette into one of the recorders, returned to the TD's chair and stared at the monitor.

When Ledyard took his place behind the podium, Ricky leaned over and drew the gooseneck-mic closer, pressed the button and said, "Okay, hold up the paper, give me 30 seconds and start talking."

As Ledyard held the paper up, Ricky saw it in the monitor, punched-up camera three, hurried into tape control, started the tape rolling and returned to the TD's chair 12 seconds before Ledyard started talking. He leaned forward and made a fine adjustment on the audio level, then turned to watch and listen as Ledyard began to relate all the unusual experiences he'd had during the last ten years of his life. Some 20 minutes later he concluded with a description of Cambian's visit in the wheel of fire and the miracle that, perhaps, would be visited upon the good Reverend Pat Patterson.

"That's quite a story," Ricky said when Ledyard strolled into the control room and tossed the paper on the counter.

"And every word of it true," Ledyard said conclusively.

"Well if it is, that's pretty weird. Weren't you scared when all that started happenin'?"

"Course I was scared, but after awhile I realized they were on my side and there was nothin' to be scared of."

"Here," Ricky held the tape out to him.

"Thanks," Ledyard said, taking the tape and tucking it under an arm. "I really appreciate you helpin' me out."

"No problem," Ricky answered, adding with a grin, "boy, you sure aren't anything like your daddy!"

Ledyard laughed, then started for the door. "See ya around."

"Wait."

"What?" Ledyard stopped and turned.

"When's this miracle supposed to happen? You didn't give a date."

Ledyard shrugged. "I don't know. My friend didn't say exactly when it would happen." He paused a moment, frowning with thought. "Tell me somethin', Ricky, and tell me the truth. If you don't believe me I won't get mad—do you?"

Ricky shrugged. "I don't know, Ledyard, but I do know *you* believe it."

Ledyard nodded. "Someday, hopefully, y'all will see it too."

CLOUD DROPS

20

A HOUSE DIVIDED

> *He that troubleth his own house shall inherit the wind: and the fool shall be servant to the wise of heart.*
> *- PROVERBS 11:29*

When Ledyard returned home from the studio, new videotape in hand, both his parents and Billy Bender were waiting for him in the formal living room. He was surprised. There was no anger, no shouting about his disappearance, just his father calling pleasantly to his son when Ledyard came in and started up the stairs.

"Yes?" Ledyard blinked as he stepped into the living room.

"You're all wet."

"Well it's raining."

"Oh." His father paused before saying with concern, "We were surprised the way you up and took off this mornin' without sayin' anything. Where'd you go?"

"Oh, I just went to see Roger at the football field."

"We know that much," his mother piped up. "He called us about 10:00 o'clock this mornin'."

"Oh?" Ledyard questioned with surprise. "What'd he say, mamma?"

"Just that he thought you were, uh, havin' some difficulties coping with reality."

Rolling his eyes, Ledyard shook his head and smiled. "Oh, well I think Roger's just, I don't know, maybe havin' some difficulties coping himself."

"What's that?" his father asked, indicating the videocassette Ledyard had tucked under one arm.

"Just a tape," he answered, holding it up. "A little project I'm workin' on."

"For school?"

"Uh, maybe."

"Maybe?" his father questioned.

"What I mean is, I might use it for a school project if it's good enough."

"Oh. Okay," the reverend smiled.

All this pleasantness was beginning to unnerve Ledyard. Something was definitely up, but before he could think to ask what, his father cleared his throat and with a glance at his wife, said, "There's someone we want you to meet."

Ledyard looked at him. "Who?"

"It's a kind of guidance counselor," his mother chirped brightly. "Someone who we think will be able to help you."

"Help me?" Ledyard turned on her with a frown. "Help me what?"

"Oh, just help you over this little period of difficulty you're goin' through."

Shaking his head, Ledyard nervously laughed. "What're y'all talkin' 'bout, mamma?"

As his father rose to his feet so did Billy Bender, all the while staring at Ledyard with just a hint of mirth.

"Here," his father said and held out his hand.

Ledyard looked at him oddly. "What?"

"The tape." It wouldn't survive the day. That evening, less than five minutes into it, the good reverend would spin it back and erase it. Every word.

Ledyard handed it to him as his mother got to her feet and took his right arm. The reverend took his left. Then they started walking for the door, Billy Bender following as Ledyard, looking from father to mother and back again, asked nervously, "What's goin' on?"

"I told you," his mother said, "there's someone in Houston we want you to meet. Someone who's goin' to help you, Ledyard."

He turned and stared at her, revealing a trace of anger as he asked, "Help me *what?*"

His mother smiled, saying gently, "Ledyard, you're a big boy now. Much too big to be scared of goin' to the doctor."

"Doctor?"

As they approached the door, Billy Bender sprang around front, popped it open as Ledyard's parents guided him through, then pulled the door closed after them and hurried to open the door of the rather plain black Lincoln the reverend had ordered for what, he hoped, would be an inconspicuous ride to Mount Pleasant Sanitarium. After the three of them were settled in back Billy firmly closed the door, went around to the driver's side, got in and started the engine.

As they drove past the guardhouse at the campus' main gate, his father said reassuringly, "Now there's nothin' to be afraid of, Ledyard. We just thought with all the pressure you're under a little rest away from here might do you some good."

"But I don't want a rest!" Ledyard insisted, beginning to get angry. "I'm not tired!"

"And that's exactly why you need a rest," his mother said. "You're so tired you don't even know it!"

"I noticed it too, Ledyard," Billy Bender put in, glancing in the rearview mirror. Ledyard glared back with naked hatred.

"Now it'll only be for a few weeks, Ledyard. Nothin' to get upset about," his father cajoled.

"But I'll miss school," the boy said. "And football."

"The team will get along just fine," his father replied.

"I know, but why're y'all doin' this to me?" Ledyard suddenly wailed.

"Ledyard!" his mother exclaimed, shocked. "We're only tryin' to help you!"

He looked at her gravely. "Help me, mamma? Help me *what?*"

The big black Lincoln bounced with a splash through the dip of the rain gutter as it turned in at the main gate, *Mount Pleasant Sanitarium* inscribed in stainless steel script on the ten-foot-high stone wall. The car continued up the blacktop drive and stopped beneath the portico with a tiny squeak from one dirty brake pad.

Two men in white coats with pleasant smiles appeared immediately, pushing through the glass doors and approaching the car. One reached out and opened the Lincoln's rear door, helped Brenda May out, and then took a firm grip on Ledyard's arm, saying as the boy emerged, "Ah, this must be the patient."

Brenda May smiled brightly, "Yes, this is Ledyard. We spoke to the doctor this mornin' and he said...."

"That's quite all right, ma'am," the orderly interjected, his smile never wavering. "We were expecting you." By now the second orderly had a firm grip on Ledyard's other arm.

"Yes, of course," Brenda May smiled, giving Ledyard a kiss on the cheek. "Now be a good boy, darlin', and do what the doctor tells you and we'll be back to visit just as soon as he says it's okay." She patted his cheek, then slipped into the car as Billy Bender sprang to and closed the door.

Ledyard glanced back once as the orderlies led him away, his mother waving from the open window as the car pulled away.

Inside, the orderlies, with Ledyard in a firm grip between them, paused at the admittance station, one saying to the nurse behind the counter, "Paperwork's been done on this one here this morning."

"Okay." She smiled warmly at Ledyard. "Name?"

"Ledyard Patterson," one of the orderlies immediately spoke up. "You know, the big-wheel preacher's son."

"Oh yes, of course," she said, noting the time of admission in her log.

Giving Ledyard a tug, the orderlies moved on, turning right at the corner and continuing down a corridor to the first door on the left. They pushed the door open, brought Ledyard inside and left, locking the door behind them.

It was a stark, windowless, linoleum-tiled room harshly illuminated with fluorescent lighting. There were several small rectangular tables, each with four chairs, and a row of four vending machines along the wall dispensing coffee and soup, soda, chips, candy and ice cream. A sign on the wall under the clock at one end of the room advised; *Clean Up After Yourself,* and beneath in smaller letters, *Everybody Likes Bacon, But Nobody Likes A Pig!*

Numb, Ledyard sank into a chair and stared at the wall with unseeing eyes. After a moment he sensed someone's presence and turned to see a bespectacled face peering through a small window in the door. Glaring back until the face disappeared, he heard keys jingling as the door was unlocked.

Tucking the keys into the pocket of his white smock, the tiny, dark-complected doctor, a native of East India with short, greasy black hair and thick eyeglasses, pulled the door open and came into the room followed by two burley black men in pale blue smocks. "Sit," the doctor curtly commanded the orderlies, indicating the farthest table. The two black men immediately complied, chairs screeching against tile as they pulled them out and sat down.

Satisfied, the doctor approached Ledyard, who was still staring at him. He stood looking down at the boy for some moments, then flipped open an aluminum chart cover, eyes scanning the page as he absently asked, "Mind if I sit down?"

"It's y'all's hospital," Ledyard quipped.

The doctor moved to the opposite side of the table and sat down, jotting *apparent hostility* in the chart. He looked up and smiled. "I am Doctor Pavlavi and I will be working closely with you in assistance to Doctor Beasely. Now," he paused, glancing down at the chart, "Ledyard? I say it right?"

Ledyard rolled his eyes with a tired sigh. After a long pause he answered, "Yeah, you got it right."

"Good. I just want to ask a few questions before the doctor gets here." Again the little man looked down at the chart, which he held angled towards himself, the back resting against the table edge, and jotted, *excessive eye movement; diminished concentration; trouble remembering name.*

"Are you hungry, Ledyard?"

"No. I feel nervous. Sick to my stomach."

"When was the last time you ate?"

When Ledyard thought about it he was shocked. Sent to bed without supper the night before, having missed breakfast that morning and in all the excitement lunch too, he hadn't eaten anything since noon the previous day. No wonder he wasn't feeling well. The thought gave him a headache, and all at once he found himself craving broiled lobster with drawn butter and a side of Minnesota-grown wild rice.

"Well?" the doctor inquired, peering closely at him.

"Noon yesterday," Ledyard answered.

The doctor jotted, *diminished appetite, gastric disturbance, nervousness, hasn't eaten in over 24 hours and claims no hunger.* He looked up and smiled, "Very well. Now, according to your parents you've been hearing voices and seeing ghosts. Could you tell me a little about this?"

Ledyard frowned, angry at the condescending attitude and saying sarcastically, "Yeah, God talks to me every day. Haven't you ever heard the expression 'like father like son?'"

The doctor's brows furrowed as he scribbled furiously on the chart, *delusions of grandeur; hears the voice of God.*

At that moment the door swung open and a tall, young-looking 42-year-old Doctor Beasely strode briskly into the room and stopped at the table. Nodding a quick, "Good afternoon, Doctor Pavlavi," to the East Indian, he extended a hand to his young patient and cheerily introduced himself. "Hi, you must be Ledyard Patterson. I'm doctor Beasely, head psychiatrist here at Mount Pleasant, and I'll be overseeing your rehabilitation and recovery with the assistance of Doctor Pavlavi here."

Ledyard looked up at the man in bewilderment, thinking, *my rehabilitation!?* which Pavlavi duly noted as *incoherent and confused* in his little chart. Lowering his eyes, Ledyard found himself staring at the man's hand like it was a claw or something and quickly looked away.

"Well then," Doctor Beasely said, withdrawing his hand. "Your parents told me you've been hearing voices, things like that. Tell me, when did this first start, Ledyard?"

"When I was six," Ledyard absently answered, staring with unseeing eyes at the tabletop.

Doctor Pavlavi scribbled *lethargic,* then looked up at Beasely and gestured that he had enough information. Glancing at him, Doctor Beasely held up a finger. "And what did God say to you, Ledyard?"

"It wasn't God," Ledyard answered in monotone, still staring with unfocused eyes at the tabletop.

"Ah, angels then?"

"No. Men. That came from heaven."

"And they told you what? That your father was undoing the work of Christ?"

When Ledyard didn't respond the doctor said quietly, "Ah, I see." He glanced at Pavlavi with an expression that brought the little East Indian out of his seat. "Will you excuse us a moment?" he said to the boy.

Barely moving his head, Ledyard nodded.

The two doctors stepped into the hall, letting the door shut behind them. Pavlavi handed his superior the chart, saying chattily, "It's all there, doctor. Hostility, diminished concentration, memory lapses, excessive eye movement, loss of appetite, hearing voices, delusions of grandeur and hallucinations."

"I see that," Beasely interjected. "Hasn't eaten in 24 hours and isn't hungry."

"Yes, with irrational hostility."

"Hmmm," shaking his head, Beasely flipped the chart closed. "Started when he was six!" He looked at Pavlavi, handing him the chart. "Imagine that!"

"Yes," Pavlavi sadly concurred. "A classic textbook case of progressive paranoid schizophrenia."

Beasely looked at his assistant, brows furrowed in thought as he asked, "How violent do you suppose he is?"

Pavlavi shrugged. "I suppose very. Have you ever seen one that wasn't? Especially considering this is his first experience with being institutionalized. You know how it is, they always react the same."

The doctor sighed. "Yes, I suppose you're right, but only use restraints if absolutely necessary."

"Of course," Pavlavi said, flipping the chart open and scribbling furiously as Beasely began dictating.

"Okay, then I suggest we start him off with five milligrams of haloperidol twice a day as an anti-psychotic agent, and 50 milligrams of thioridazine three times a day to calm him. After we see how he responds to that we'll decide on our maintenance dosage."

"Very good, doctor," Pavlavi said, flipping the chart closed.

"Then I'll leave him in your most capable hands, doctor," Beasely said and started off down the corridor.

Pavlavi immediately pulled the door open and poked his head in, saying, "Okay, Ledyard, would you come with me?"

Ledyard looked up and stared dully at the man. Immediately the two orderlies got to their feet, moved to either side of Ledyard, took him under the armpits and hauled him to his feet, one saying threateningly, "Now, you wanna walk or you wanna be dragged?"

Ledyard looked at the man and by way of answering, tried pulling his arms free.

"Okay, puppy," the big man said, "let's go."

They moved so suddenly and quickly Ledyard stumbled. Refusing to pause long enough to allow him to regain his footing, and ignoring his cries to be let go, the orderlies dragged him the entire length of the corridor. The petite doctor followed with quick little steps like he was on wheels, scribbling in his precious chart, *uncooperative, refuses to walk.*

At the admittance station the group turned right down a short corridor where one orderly unlocked a security door. Beyond was more corridor with doors on either side. "C-8," Pavlavi instructed. "I can see this one will need restraints."

At C-8 the orderlies unlocked the door. The tiny, barren room contained nothing but a single bed with leather restraints at each corner and a small, dirty window with bars near the ceiling. As the orderlies bound Ledyard spread-eagled on his back on the bed, Pavlavi stood nearby looking down at him sympathetically, saying in a kindly voice, "You see, Ledyard? Fighting us will only result in your further discomfort. All we want to do is make you well."

"But I'm not sick!" Ledyard shouted in furious frustration.

"Then why are you fighting and shouting?" the doctor calmly asked. "If you weren't sick you wouldn't be fighting and shouting at those trying to help you."

This made Ledyard even more furious, causing him to fling his head from side to side, the only movement possible with the restraints binding him hand and foot. At last he stopped, breathing heavily with rage as he looked angrily at Pavlavi, who calmly continued. "Now, doctor Beasely has ordered some medications for you, but often patients refuse to take the pills or spit them out and then we have to pull their pants down and use a needle." He paused, looking at Ledyard, then asked quietly, "Will you take the pills or should I get my hypodermic needle?"

"But I don't need to be drugged!" Ledyard hotly protested. "There's nothing wrong with me!"

The doctor shook his head. "But don't you see, Ledyard? That right there is a symptom of your mental illness. No one here ever wants to take their medication. That's why they're sick. If you would take your medications you wouldn't be sick. Trust me. I know. I'm a doctor. Take them and you'll see. In a few days you'll be feeling much better. Your appetite will come back and you'll feel calm and in control of your emotions."

It was no use. And he certainly didn't want this mealy-mouthed little rodent pulling *his* pants down and sticking needles in God only knew where. Fighting back tears of humiliation and frustration, Ledyard turned and stared at the wall, saying in a shaky voice filled with despair, "Okay, bring the pills."

CLOUD DROPS

21

HEAVEN CAN'T WAIT

> *And there was given him dominion, and glory, and a kingdom, that all people, nations, and languages should serve him: his dominion is an everlasting dominion, which shall not pass away, and his kingdom that which shall not be destroyed.*
> *- DANIEL 7:14*

As the drama on Earth was building, the crowds in the House of Kings were growing larger and more vocal. Some had witnessed Ledyard's internment in the psychiatric ward on the SuperViewer and word had gotten around. Now, before the crowded chamber with the spokesman of the gray team at his side, Jesus was refereeing a lively debate over whether to continue with the "Patterson Plan" or drop it like a hot potato. At the moment Gautoma Buddha was arguing that since Ledyard had utterly failed to move the Reverend Pat Patterson one iota the project should be abandoned immediately. After all, under the circumstances it seemed unlikely that further efforts would have any beneficial results.

"What? And just abandon this boy to the insane asylum after he put himself, his reputation and everything else on the line for us?" Susan Brownell Anthony cried indignantly and leapt to her feet. "Not on your life!" The nineteenth century American pioneer of women's rights gazed around the gathered forum and added with finality, "I say on to the next phase of the plan!" Without further ado she took her seat to a smattering of applause. The issue was by no means settled.

Malcolm X, who happened to be sitting next to Martin Luther King, leaned close, whispering, "Think I'll sit this one out."

"Not me," Doctor King said and stood up. Turning to address the original suffragette, he bowed slightly with just the trace of a smile and said, "Now, I don't want anyone to get the mistaken impression that I'm saying this just because they put Ms. Anthony's face on an American coin, but I totally agree with her position. After all, the boy *did* back us, now it's our turn to back *him.*" About to take his seat, Martin suddenly straightened again, adding with a nod to Malcolm, "By any means necessary!" and sat down to louder, more widespread applause, the pro-faction apparently gaining ground.

"I'm with Susan and Martin," Mohammed called from his seat, "the time for action is now!"

Glancing at Jesus, Cambian decided to make his move and stepped forward. "The 'means' Doctor King spoke of is by way of a miracle," he asserted. "As some of you may know, the miracle I am speaking of is the code-six we talked about some ten years ago when we initiated the 'Patterson Plan.' Namely, my appearance in the flesh."

"But the boy we have convinced," Ghandi said, getting to his feet, "what purpose would it serve now?"

"I'm not concerned about convincing the boy," Cambian replied. "I was thinking about convincing the reverend and his congregation. Imagine the shock value if I suddenly appear in the flesh before him and his whole congregation. With all the previous preparation Ledyard has provided it just might jar the reverend into a complete and total conversion along with the entire congregation. Then we'd *really* be in a position to express our views."

Now Malcolm X stood up, proclaiming with loud boldness, "And if the reverend decides you're hell-sent instead of heaven-bent? And likewise manages to convince his TV audience of millions? By the time it's all over the whole nation may be holding this hypocritical money-monger in reverence. It could even transcend international boundaries, which would certainly set us back—probably *permanently!*" Malcolm snatched his robes about him and sat down, the forum deathly silent.

After a moment Jesus spoke up. "I tend to agree with Malcolm. Besides," he lamented, "I hate miracles like this. They never seem to work."

"We anticipated the possibility of the miracle backfiring," Cambian replied, turning briefly to Jesus, then to the audience at large. "And the team and I have come up with a perfect plan to avert just such a disaster."

He paused, composing his thoughts, then continued. "Right before I make my appearance the rest of the team will deflect the microwave television signal into space so it misses the relayer, effectively disrupting the broadcast entirely. And there won't be a thing the technicians can do about it until my team gives them back their signal. Now, if the previously mentioned disaster does occur, well, it'll be limited to the 5,000 or so audience members in attendance. Even if my appearance is caught on tape, to the now video-wise world it will simply look like a cleverly executed jump-cut and when, or if, they present their 'evidence' of having witnessed a miracle the world will just laugh at them, their ratings very likely plummeting. And we certainly wouldn't be any the worse off for *that!*"

Jesus was impressed. For the audience's sake he turned to Cambian. "And the benefit to us," he asked, "if the

miracle succeeds in winning over the reverend and his congregation?"

"Well," Cambian paused, "then we may not have the
world, but we'll certainly have 5,000 devoted apostles and
a fiery preacher to help spread the word. *Our* word!" he
concluded to thunderous applause.

*   *   *

When Cambian got home he found his teammates playing in the pool. Although they could have gone to the
debate, they had elected to spend their leisure time having
fun. Simply put, they hadn't been interested in listening to
a bunch of old-timers argue the pros, cons, and rightful
functions of miracle-casting. Whatever was decided, they'd
be doing it regardless.

But they were anxious to know the outcome. And for
the sheer fun of being a party to executing it, everyone was
hoping the decision would go in favor of the miracle. So
when Cambian came out the backdoor onto the patio they
dropped what they were doing, scrambled out of the pool
and crowded around jabbering excitedly.

"Whoa! Whoa!" Cambian laughed, holding up his
hands. With everyone's excitement barely contained he
shouted, "We're on!" Cheering and leaping for joy, a free-
for-all ensued as the team started throwing each other into
the pool.

That evening after a celebratory meal they went to bed
early in excited anticipation of the morning's flight out.
Tomorrow was Sunday and it had been decided that the
Sunday evening service when, supposedly, the preacher
would be feeling his most holy and humble, would be the
best time to make their move.

For Cambian and his three girls it would be their last night together for God-only-knew how long, and they spent the entire night in a long session of lovemaking, only taking an hour of "dreamphase."

The fact that Cambian would soon be taken from his lovers for, perhaps, decades, was not at all disturbing to them. Natalie, Michelle, and Debbie would simply be taken in by other "families." And although they would miss him, to these eternal creatures even a hundred years would pass in the blink of an eye. Furthermore, they wouldn't be dealing with the apprehension Earthlings experience when they must part for extended periods because, unlike their Earthbound counterparts, they *know* they'll be reunited with their loved ones.

*   *   *

Streaking south over Tulsa, Oklahoma the following evening after having dropped the girls, the remainder of the gray team spotted Other Ones clustered around the vicinity of Doral Doberts University like flies around an outhouse. At rest, the pale yellowish glow of their spherical bodies was clearly visible to the team even though totally invisible to the human subjects they were attempting to "channel" to.

The fires of their souls flaring from cruising-orange to hot-blue, the team arced around in a tight circle for a closer look, Cambian saying, "Looks like Dicky Doberts must be preparing his Sunday evening sermon. Should we run them Lunar Ticks off?"

"Lunar Ticks" was their nickname for Other Ones. Within the scope of Earth's atmosphere they were fair game for the Elite, who could deliver a painful shock that Other Ones were deathly afraid of. It rarely came to that, though, as the panic-stricken Other Ones usually scrambled to the safety of the dark side of the moon, in which case the rescue squad would call off the chase satisfied at having routed them. Otherwise they would just as soon not even get close, let alone *touch* them. A repulsive proposition indeed.

"We got the time, my man," Avery replied.

"Doesn't matter much whether we run them off or not," James put in. "That Doberts clan seems good enough at misguiding themselves even without the help of the Lunar Ticks."

Andy laughed, commenting, "I like the one they gave Doral about the 958 and three-quarter-foot Jesus!"

"I like the one about 'Give me eight and three-quarter million bucks or God is gonna call me home,'" Avery laughed. "You'd think the man would've had sense enough not to have bitten on that one!"

"Well, let's do it," Cambian said, and then the team pitched into a steep, screaming dive, the four revolving wheels of the "disc" glowing a fiery bluish-white as they dropped through the mists of the mare's tail clouds, the twinkling lights of Tulsa, Oklahoma far below.

The Other Ones "heard" them coming and looked up, startled, and immediately scattered for the moon.

With the Other Ones routed, the gray team leveled off at 65,000 feet and continued south towards Houston at a very leisurely 500 mph. Thus would they arrive refreshed and ready for the big one.

"Right on time," Avery said as they swooped in low over the Christian Condensed Ministry's campus and hovered near the television studio's microwave satellite transmitter.

"Now you guys know what to do, right?" Cambian asked.

"Right," Andy answered. "We're just going to join hands in a semicircle, position ourselves in the beam and deflect it off into space."

"You got a fix on the satellite, James?" Cambian asked, turning to him.

"Got it," came the reply.

"Now don't forget," Cambian cautioned, "we want to *miss* the satellite."

"Right," his three companions answered in unison.

"After I'm inside wait for my okay before releasing the broadcast beam."

"Will-Co Roger," James said.

"All right, guess this is goodbye then."

This was it. They very likely wouldn't be seeing Cambian again for many years. He was taking on the flesh and would die in the flesh. However long it took.

Everyone crowded around for a last embrace, Cambian cautioning, "Now don't forget, take your position, keep your eye on me, and be ready to move. But don't make your move until the moment you see me make mine. I'll move slow so you get in ahead of me and broadcast interruption occurs just before I appear inside the auditorium. Okay?"

"Got it," his three friends answered, the love and admiration they felt for him clearly revealed in their faces.

All of them, including Cambian, were experiencing "butterflies" as the lone operative dropped from the ship and slowly descended, glancing back once with a wave as his companions assembled at their battle station.

Taking a position over the portion of roof above the stage, Cambian "radioed" his teammates, "All set?"

"Roger."

"Okay," Cambian hesitated, "let's move!" And then he vanished through the roof.

CLOUD DROPS

22

IN THE FLESH

> *...For thou wast slain, and hast redeemed us to God by thy blood out of **every kindred, and tongue, and people, and nation**....*
> *- REVELATIONS 5:9*

In the dim coolness of the control room aglow with the bluish cast of eight television monitors, the director sat staring at only one as he began counting down into his headset: "Five, four, three, two, one—roll tape!"

At his station in tape control Ricky Brown, finger at the ready, punched a button and called out sharply, "Rolling!"

The announcer's voice came through loud in the control room as a computer-generated graphic spun up on the screen entitled *Christian Condensed Ministries* with the logo in the middle and the famous slogan parenthesized underneath, *(Just Add Blood And Stir!)*. The background was a montage of shots of a strutting, sweating, tearful, ranting, raving Pat Patterson.

"Fade music, dissolve to three," the director spoke rapidly.

On the program monitor a huge auditorium with a wildly applauding audience filled the screen as a trim Pat Patterson, perfect hair and cherubic cheeks as rosy as a baby's behind, stepped from the wings. Nattily attired in a dark suit, red-striped tie and clutching a Bible, he strode across the immense, rounded stage carpeted in royal-blue and took his place at stage center behind the podium.

As the applause died he laid the Bible down, opened it to a place previously marked and leaned towards the mic. Hesitating until the audience was perched on the edges of their seats in anxious anticipation, he began in a solemn, dispassionate voice, "My 16-year-old son came to me last week with a videotape he'd recently made. A videotape on which he described what he believed to be his experiences with the supernatural." (A videotape, the good reverend failed to mention, that, aside from the opening comments, he had not viewed.) "Now, over the years as he was growin' up he would come to me with some tale or another about God or angels or whatnot comin' to him with messages — messages that he was supposed to deliver to me."

"Ohhh," the exclamation of wounded surprise rose to the middle of the packed auditorium and died off at the sides.

"Now, when this all started he was just a young'n, and a very imaginative one I might add, so I wasn't too concerned — at first." He glanced up at the ceiling briefly, uttering, "Forgive me, Lord, I should have been more attentive," then returned his gaze to the audience. "Anyway, as his..." he faltered, *"illness,* for lack of a better term, progressed, I took him aside on several occasions and usin' THIS BOOK!" he suddenly shouted, hoisting the Bible aloft, pages aflutter as he dropped it back on the podium with a loud *thump,* "I pointed out to him the gross scriptural contradictions in the messages his angel friends were givin' him.

"But no, daddy, the boy argued with me, twistin' the words of THIS BOOK," he hoisted the Bible again, "to suit his own fantasies! And when you argue with THIS BOOK," he continued to shout, waving the Bible in the air, "then you're arguin' with God!" he concluded in a deep guttural voice, leaning forward and shaking his head like a dog with a piece of meat.

He straightened up, tossing the Bible on the podium, started off to the left, put his hands to the sides of his head like a man in great anguish, pivoted, strode back to the podium, snatched the mic from its holder and slumped, heaving a loud sigh directly into the mic. At last he looked up, acute pain etched on his face. "I wasn't goin' to tell you this," he thumped the podium. "And I'm not goin' to carry on about it, but I would be less than honest if I didn't tell the whole story." His head suddenly jerked back as he cried to the heavens, "OH GOD FORGIVE ME I NEED TO TELL SOMEONE!"

There was a long sniffling silence. The beads of sweat on his face and dribbling down his cheeks could well have been tears. Head bowed and heaving a shaky sigh, he pulled a hanky from his pocket and dabbed at his face, muttering, "I caught my son in a homosexual act with another boy."

Confused audience members turned to one another unsure if they had heard right. Amid the growing hiss of questioning whispers they were suddenly startled to attention when the reverend howled in a wounded voice, "I SAID I CAUGHT MY SON IN A HOMOSEXUAL ACT WITH ANOTHER BOY!"

A veritable roar of "Ooohs!" and "Ahhhs!" rippled through the crowd.

The preacher shuffled to the edge of the stage, face sagging as he said in a voice thick with grief, "Shortly thereafter I began to watch my son disintegrate into madness." And then he folded into himself, chin on his chest, shoulders shaking as he broke down sobbing.

Sad-eyed members of the audience dabbed at tears. Others clasped hands, murmuring with eyes closed and faces raised to the ceiling beseeching deliverance on behalf of their preacher from the horrible pain they felt sure was ripping at the core of his heart.

After a moment he looked up, dabbing at his own tears, then swabbed his face and blew his nose. At last dry, voice stabilized, the reverend said, "And that's when I witnessed my son, my dear, dear Ledyard, begin his insane pursuit to displace me. To gain power and wealth through evil."

He strode back to the podium again, some apparently invisible force seeming to surge through him bringing new life. "It is only conjecture on my part, of course," he continued. "I can only imagine what was goin' through his mind as, day after day, he began his attack on the holy word of God and *me,* his own daddy." He nodded several times. "Yes, I can only imagine what fantasies his sick mind must have been entertainin' as he conspired with demons to depose me and take over this ministry!"

He was starting to shout again, excitedly spinning on his heel to do one of his strutting numbers when to his awestruck wonder there was a loud *pfhhht!* and out of thin air right before his ever widening and disbelieving eyes there appeared a brown-eyed little oriental boy with longish black hair, naked and barefoot except for a skimpy pair of gray cotton shorts with three interlocking blue rings on the hip.

In the moment of stunned silence that followed, the startled preacher dropped the microphone. It banged off the floor with a loud screech of feedback. White as a ghost, eyes locked on the boy, the trembling preacher stooped and snatched up the mic as the roar from the audience grew deafening. Wild-eyed like a frightened horse, he fought down a terrifying impulse to reach out and touch the boy, to see if he was real. Drunk with fear and confusion, he backed up, stumbling into the podium, mouth opening and closing wordlessly as he grabbed on like a man drowning.

His wife and the church elders sitting in a special roped-off section in the front might have leapt to the stage and his aid but they were no longer even aware they had feet. Slack-jawed, they sat staring. It just couldn't be. But it was.

Sagging against the podium, supported by one arm thrown across the top and gripping the front edge, the preacher suddenly felt like his head was an empty, swollen, air-filled bulb. With great effort he twisted his eyes from the boy and turned to stare drunkenly at the roaring audience which had apparently gone insane. Except for those lying fainted in the aisles or collapsed in their seats, 5,000 people, from elderly fat ladies in print dresses to stiff-collared old white men and teenagers, were standing on their upholstered chairs screaming, chanting, fists in the air, some babbling incoherently, others with their hands clasped above their heads howling at the ceiling for the precious blood of Jesus to rain down.

The preacher, his head wobbling on his shoulders like it might fall off and bounce from the stage, turned back to see if the strange little brown creature with black hair and slanted eyes was still there. By God it was! On the verge of collapse, he would have when through the fog of his whirling mind he heard a voice... a heavenly voice... faintly echoing above the roar of the crowd. "Reverend Patterson! Reverend Patterson!"

All at once the preacher snapped to. God! It was God and *he* was calling *him!* "I'm here, Lord!" Patterson cried, tears of joy running down his cheeks and dribbling off his chin. He was standing ramrod straight now, the mic gripped in two hands, head thrown back as he cried again, "Here am I, Lord!"

To the people in the front row focus and sensibility swiftly returned at the familiar sight of their preacher, mic in hand, crying out from the stage. Thus shocked from their madness and embarrassed to find themselves standing mindlessly on their chairs in their Sunday best, they quickly climbed down and took their seats.

When the people in front sat down the ones behind, now able to see, experienced a similar moment of embarrassing self-recognition and the madness swiftly abated. Like rows of dominoes fanning out across the auditorium, they started sitting down, the collective roar of 5,000 straining vocal cords vanishing like a puff of smoke.

In a sudden explosion of rattling reverberation the voice of "God" boomed out over the giant public address speakers in the ceiling, "Reverend Patterson! Reverend Patterson!"

"Yes! Yes, Lord! I hear you!" the preacher cried, flinging salty sweat from his gleaming brow.

There was a long pause before the booming voice once again rattled the ceiling fixtures. "No, sir. It's Tommy G., the director. We've lost transmission, sir. We're not broadcasting."

The bewildered preacher almost rocked off his rocker again until the words "we're not broadcasting" snapped him back. "Turn down the public address and stop shouting!" Issuing this order cemented his relationship with reality. All at once he knew who he was—Commander of the Godship Patterson.

"Can you hear me now, sir?" Tommy G. asked.

"Yes, that's fine, Tommy."

"What in the world is going on down there?"

"You didn't see what happened?" the reverend asked incredulously.

Cambian was standing there feeling just as weird as anyone in the room with his new body made of meat.

Sensations long forgotten, the slight tremor of his nervous system and the blood thumping through his chest, were very apparent. And these meat units didn't come fueled, either, he suddenly realized, experiencing his first hunger pangs. And *cold!* Then something weird in his shorts moved. Startled, he pulled the waistband away from his stomach and peeked inside. Of course! He had *balls*. And more.

"I didn't see anything, sir. Just before all hell broke... I mean, started screaming, we had total transmission failure and I was frantically trying to resolve it."

"Well are we transmittin' now?"

"No sir. It's still out. I've got the engineers working on it but I've never seen them like this before. They're completely baffled. They say the signal's going out but it's not reaching the satellite relayer."

"Well then there's somethin' wrong with the satellite," the reverend replied sharply.

"No sir, that's the odd thing. All the other stations are operating fine, it's only *our* station that's experiencing the disruption, so it can't be the satellite, sir."

"Hmmm," the reverend pondered. "Then it's got to be our transmitter."

A long silence followed. When Tommy G. finally replied his voice sounded strangely disturbed. "The engineers are standing right here and they're saying there's nothing detectable wrong with our equipment. It's transmitting perfectly."

"Well fix it!" the preacher roared.

"T-There's nothing to fix, sir." A long pause. "The engineers tell me it's one for the history books." Another long pause. "They tell me it's some kind of miracle. No rational explanation."

"A miracle?" the reverend questioned, looking up at the little strip of mirrored glass in the second story of the left wall. "That's the second miracle this evenin'!" he exulted.

Meanwhile the audience was sitting transfixed, listening to all of this and watching the little brown "alien" exploring his new body. To them he appeared to be an adolescent boy of no more than 14. In the interest of relating to Ledyard, Cambian had generated for himself a 16-year-old's body. The same body nature had generated for him originally. But his boyish good looks, short stature and slight, if muscular build gave him a much younger appearance.

The PA clicked on and a new voice took over. "Sir, this is chief engineer Roland Smith. I've been with you since we inaugurated this broadcast station 21 years ago." He paused. "And I worked for CBS in the same capacity for ten years before that, and in 31 years, sir, I have never seen anything like this. It just doesn't make sense. It's as if God himself reached down his mighty hand and snatched our signal. Furthermore, I want you to know that I would personally testify in any court or forum in the world that what we have here is a bona fide miracle. There's simply no other explanation." The PA clicked off.

The Reverend Pat Patterson, a look of odd curiosity on his face, slowly turned to gaze out at his audience. Almost to himself he inquired, "Is everyone else hearin' the same thing I'm hearin'?"

"YES!!" the audience roared.

"Did everyone in this room *see* the same thing I saw?" he asked, glancing at the strange creature that had appeared out of thin air.

"YES!!" the audience roared again.

"Bear with me another moment, folks." Turning to Cambian, he added, "And please, son, don't you go anywhere either!"

Cambian looked up with a friendly smile and nodded, one hand in his shorts absently exploring his new body.

Still harboring a profound sense of disbelief, the reverend grimaced, shook his head and turned back to the little strip of mirrored window high above the auditorium. "Are you still with me, Tommy G.?"

"Of course, sir."

"Did you manage to get it on tape?"

"Tape never stopped rolling, sir."

"Yes, but is this, this *thing* on tape?" he gestured at Cambian impatiently.

"What thing is that, sir?" came the perplexed reply.

"The little Chinese boy standing here naked on the stage!" the reverend bellowed hoarsely.

There was a long pause as the director apprised himself of the situation, then the click of the PA. "Uh, let me check on that for you, sir. I'll have to spin the tape back and have a look. Won't take a minute."

The director and crew had been hard at work when Cambian appeared off-camera and none of the technicians had actually witnessed the miracle save the producer, who happened to be looking out the window when the miracle occurred. But in the frantic whirlwind of activity following signal-failure no one even noticed the producer sitting there stunned as if his plug had been pulled. Only now, as the producer excitedly related what he had seen did the crew begin to get an inkling of the utter magnitude of what had happened. Now the madness that had briefly swept the auditorium was beginning to make frightening sense.

"Well hurry up and get the tape spun back!" the reverend snapped. Then he turned to Cambian, who was standing there gazing at him curiously. Looking the boy up and down with furrowed brow, he leaned towards him, asking softly, "Do you speak english?"

Cambian nodded. "Of course."

For a moment the evangelist didn't know what to say. He smiled. "Well, since you just popped in from out of this world I thought it might do to ask." He turned to the audience with a bemused smile and growing confidence. He had his wits about him now. He was ready for anything. "What do all of you make of this?" he asked rhetorically. "I-I'm," he shrugged. "For the first time in my life I'm speechless." Stepping back from the podium, he said seriously, "I mean, God has blessed *us* with a miracle. Two if you count the transmission failure!"

The audience responded with cries of "Praise the Lord!" and "Precious blood of Jesus!"

The click and hum of the PA intruded, followed by Tommy G. saying, "Sir, we've checked the tape. The boy's not on it."

"Why not?" the preacher asked sharply.

"The camera was on *you,* sir, where it belonged."

"Oh." Frowning, the reverend gazed around his congregation of 5,000. "Ladies and gentlemen, do you realize what we have here?" he asked softly, nodding his head. "The greatest miracle the modern world has ever known," he paused, almost hissing, "and we have no proof!"

He opened his mouth to continue when the click of the PA once again interrupted. "Sir, the engineer requests permission to shut down the transmitter for a closer look."

Lost in thought, pacing slowly about, the reverend glanced up. "Yes. Yes, that's fine. In fact it should probably be taken as a sign from God. Obviously he doesn't want the world to know about this. Shut it down and leave it down,

Tommy, and don't start it up again until I give the word. Okay?"

"Roger."

"Oh, and you will be recordin' everything on tape, right?"

"We're rolling tape right now, sir."

"Good. We need to save whatever happens next for posterity."

"Of course, sir." The PA clicked off.

He turned back to Cambian briefly, then the audience. "Ah, let's see now, where were we? Oh yes, we've established that our little Chinese friend speaks...."

"I'm not Chinese," Cambian interjected. "I'm Cambodian."

With arched brow the reverend turned on him. "Oh, from Cambodia are we?"

"No sir, I'm *from* heaven, but my nationality is Cambodian."

Pondering a moment, the preacher said, "Okay, let me clarify this. You were born and raised in Cambodia, died, went to heaven, and have now returned with a message for *us?* That is, for the Christian Condensed Ministry's reverend and his congregation?"

"That's correct," Cambian replied with a grin.

Giving him a sideways glance, the preacher was looking at the congregation when he asked, "And what's the big grin about?" He turned back to the "alien."

Cambian shrugged, "I just didn't think you would get it so easily."

At that the reverend laughed lightly, intoning, "Well I wouldn't start celebratin' your success too soon. I mean, you haven't convinced *me* of anything, young man."

He paused, pulling a hanky from his pocket and dabbing at his damp forehead, sniffed once, cleared his throat and asked pleasantly of the boy, "Tell me something, does everyone in heaven dress as you do? I mean, walk around in public in their underdrawers?"

Again Cambian shrugged. "Well, no. Actually, no one gives much thought to clothes at all. In fact what you see here is my entire wardrobe. But it's nice for traveling because I never have to pack a suitcase!" He laughed before adding, "Really, though, in heaven clothes are a mere formality. Most of the time we don't wear anything at all."

"You're tellin' me," he was looking quickly from Cambian to the congregation and back again, "that in heaven everyone walks around buck-neckid?"

"Well, our bodies are different than yours," Cambian struggled to explain. "Our energy field *is* our clothes, sort of." At that the congregation roared with laughter.

"Can you believe this guy?" the grinning preacher asked, shaking his head as he turned to the congregation. "Everyone in heaven walkin' around stark neckid?" He turned back to Cambian. "Well I trust they have separate quarters for the men and women," he chuckled.

"Oh no," Cambian answered, "we all sleep together."

"You all *sleep* together!?" the stunned preacher exclaimed, the congregation gasping in horror.

"Well of course," Cambian replied matter-of-factly. "Everyone sleeps with their girlfriends, mostly."

"Girl*friends?*" the reverend inquired skeptically. "Just how many girl*friends* do you have?"

"Well, not counting all the girls on our team, I have three that I pretty much sleep with every night, except when they meet some guy they like and go off with him." Grinning, he added with a wink, "But they always come back!"

The preacher looked absolutely dumbfounded. The congregation was deathly quiet, huffy, indignant looks on their faces.

Cambian was beginning to realize he wasn't making much headway. And he was also beginning to get an inkling of why Jesus wasn't so hot on miracles. But he still had an ace in the hole. Or so he thought. He looked up at the tall, fair, blue-eyed man that towered over him and asked, "What about Ledyard? Where's Ledyard?"

The preacher turned slowly, beady-eyed and suspicious. "You know my son?"

Cambian nodded enthusiastically. "And he would recognize me, sir, I just know he would. Didn't he tell you about when I visited him?"

"That was *you?* Oh, he told me about it all right! And he's in the hospital right now driven insane by homosexual and demonic forces."

All at once struck with a disturbing insight, the reverend turned to pacing about the stage, eyes downcast, face creased with a dark frown. If all of this were true then everything Ledyard had been telling him all along was right. And everything he himself taught was absolutely wrong. And if *that* were true....

In a flash the Reverend Pat Patterson saw all his wealth and power evaporating. Driven by this single, gnawing fear, it was then that he made up his mind. This kid couldn't be a messenger from God. No way. He had to be the devil. Or the son of the devil. And Patterson was going to do something about it. He stopped pacing and for a moment couldn't quite believe what he was about to say. But by God it was true! It had to be.

"Then you're the one!" Patterson cried hoarsely and spun on his heel to face the congregation. "Ladies and gentlemen, I would like to introduce to you my son's demonic spiritual guide. *In the flesh!"*

He paused to look the boy up and down, then turned abruptly to the congregation and screeched, "Scripture tells us even Satan himself can appear as an angel of light! Now I ask you, does this sound like, *look* like, a miracle from heaven, or a miracle from hell?"

"HELL!" the audience roared.

"Ah, yes," the preacher smiled, waving a hand over the congregation like he was giving a benediction. "There's a flock of sheep that knows their shepherd!"

"Sir!" Cambian called to the man's back. "Sir, I know what you're getting at," he continued when the man turned, "and that's why we deflected your broadcast signal off the satellite." He held up a finger, "One moment."

Staring straight ahead, apparently in deep concentration, Cambian frowned, placing the fingers of both hands to his temples. He was "radioing" his teammates, but the meat he had suddenly found himself so heavily encased in was muffling the transmission, like static on the radio when a car drives behind a mountain. All at once Cambian looked up with a smile, saying cheerfully, "In fact I can assure you that your transmitter should work perfectly now if you want to resume your broadcast."

"You're quite sure about that, are you?"

"Quite sure, yes."

"Well in case you haven't noticed, *I'm* the one callin' the shots here and I'll decide when we resume broadcastin'!" He paused, catching his breath. "Because, you see, I don't believe you came down from heaven. I believe you came up from hell!"

"AMEN! PRAISE THE LORD!" and "PRECIOUS BLOOD OF JESUS!" echoed throughout the cavernous auditorium.

"And furthermore," Patterson continued sharply, "if this was the Lord's work, *his* miracle, he would not have shorted-out the broadcast. On the contrary, he would have broadcast it to all the world! Otherwise," he concluded to thunderous applause, "to what purpose the miracle? We don't have an ounce of proof!"

Heaving a sigh, Cambian shook his head. Then realized something. Maybe if the congregation could hear *him* too... He walked over to where the preacher was standing at the edge of the stage and tapped him on the shoulder.

Startled, Patterson whirled around shouting, "Security! Security! He touched me! Get up here *now!*"

Cambian resisted an amused smile, saying, "Nothing to get upset about. I just wanted to explain something."

But the reverend only stared at him, warily backing away and bellowing shrilly, "Don't touch me!"

In the meantime two blue-suited security personnel hurried up the center aisle, hustled on stage and grabbed Cambian's arms. Yanking the boy around to face the audience, the guards looked to their reverend for instruction.

"Handcuff him!" the preacher ordered.

Immediately one guard twisted the boy's arms up behind his back while the other snapped the cuffs on.

"Okay, turn him loose."

The guards let him go and stepped back two paces.

Feeling a whole lot safer, the preacher smiled pleasantly, cocked his head to one side and said, "Now *that* should teach you to keep your hands to yourself!"

This whole thing was beginning to lose its appeal for Cambian. "I just wanted to explain about something!" he said harshly, and then realized with a start that anger was a whole other emotion. Something else he had entirely forgotten about.

"Okay, fine," the preacher smiled, nodding once, "Please proceed."

"About interrupting the broadcast," Cambian continued. "You see, the Lord doesn't trust miracles. In fact he hates doing them. He says they never work."

"Ho-ho!" the preacher shouted with a hearty laugh like Santa. "Jesus hates miracles! They never work! Did you hear that?" he asked the audience, his head bobbing back and forth as he stepped around the podium and walked to the forward edge of the stage.

With a sharp gesture at Cambian he continued. "Our little Oriental friend here claims the God of Moses, the one who parted the Red Sea and led the nation of Israel through the desert by a column of fire which carried the finger of God carving the Ten Commandments in stone, hates doing miracles because they never work!"

The congregation roared with laughter and applauded.

He was getting back into his old fire-and-brimstone form now and enjoying it immensely. "Well I don't know what kind of Bible you've been reading, kid, but *my* Bible is filled with countless tales of successful miracles!"

Cambian shrugged, saying conversationally, "Well, actually, I've never read the Bible. Most of my understanding of God came through the Buddhist tradition when I was growing up in Cambodia."

At that the auditorium grew deathly quiet, every eye on the darkly exotic, lean, muscular Oriental youth that stood handcuffed before them. As far as they were concerned he was a black panther escaped from the zoo of hell.

The preacher, feet firmly planted, twisted around to stare at the boy, and almost whispered, "You're going to stand there and tell me you died a Buddhist, went to heaven, and have now returned to Earth on behalf of Jesus Christ?"

He turned back to the audience. "Can you believe *that,* ladies and gentlemen?"

There was just a moment's hesitation before the audience roared, "NO!"

"And how do we know that?" the preacher roared back almost as loudly with the aid of his microphone. From the audience came a weak smattering of replies as they searched their stiff and brittle brains for the scripture and verse-number they knew their preacher was looking for.

"Oh how quickly we forget!" he smiled big at the congregation, then shouted at the top of his lungs, "John 14:6 tells us verbatim, 'I am the way, the truth, and the life. No man cometh unto the Father but by me!'" He jerked a thumb over his shoulder at Cambian, proclaiming hoarsely, "He's just confessed before you, me, and everybody else that he's nothin' more than a Satan-worshipin' Buddhist come straight from hell!" He was getting fierce-eyed and sweaty now as he strode about the stage clutching his mic.

At last he stopped, straightening up, his voice thick with phlegm and strain, "Ladies and gentlemen, I give you the Antichrist, whom God hath placed safely and surely in our hands!"

The preacher paused for a long, dramatic moment, completely lost in his fear-generated delusion, then whispered into the mic while leaning forward at the waist and wagging his head, "And that makes *us* the first 5,000 of the 144,000! Or perhaps," he hastened to add, "the priests that judge the 12 tribes of Israel!"

At that the congregation exploded into wild cheering.

Getting nervous, Cambian stood shivering with one foot on the other. It was a hot October evening in southern Texas and he wasn't at all used to air conditioning. He felt like he was standing naked in a giant refrigerator with some very strange creatures as weird and scary as any he had encountered in all his travels through the galaxies. And then he was thunderstruck with a thought. *These were his own people!* From a different neighborhood of the world, maybe, but still Earthlings, just like him! Moses had been right. Lost in his thoughts, he laughed when he remembered this was supposedly going to be an easy job with big-ticket credit.

And then Patterson was in his face with his mic, flecks of spittle hitting Cambian as the preacher screeched, "He's laughin' at us! Listen!"

Cambian just eyed the man coldly.

In a rising sing-song the preacher said, "I don't hear anything!" He straightened abruptly and turned back to the congregation. "Well, I guess he must have felt the glow of God all around me when I got near and it scared him!"

The audience laughed and applauded, he nodding appreciation as if he'd just performed a major miracle. "The question is, my priestly brothers and sisters," he intoned, striding a circle about his prey, "what to do with him?"

"Call immigration!" one portly gentleman with rosy cheeks and white hair shouted from the third row, which generated light laughter from that portion of the massive audience who heard the comment.

"Did you hear that, ladies and gentlemen?" the preacher asked rhetorically. "A fella down here in front says to call immigration!" He glanced at Cambian, "And then you *know* what would happen. Eventually he'd be released. And then we will have been responsible for loosing the Antichrist into the world!" He dabbed at the sweat beading up on his forehead and asked loudly, "Do we want that?"

"NO!" the congregation roared.

"Well what should we do with him?" the preacher asked again, strolling easily about the front of the stage. He eyed a man in the second row, prompting him, but it didn't work this time. The man merely held up his hands in a gesture indicating he honestly had no idea.

"We can't call the police either, because technically this little whatever-it-is doesn't really exist. True? I mean we all sat right here and saw him just *poof!* right into our lives out of thin air!"

He turned and stopped beside Cambian, gesturing at the little forlorn creature far below him, which he viewed as even less than a cockroach. "Nobody's ever gonna miss somebody that was never here to begin with," he said quietly, at this point totally deluded and thoroughly insulated from reality by the bubble of his own bloated ego.

A murmuring quickly spread through the auditorium as the preacher continued building his case. "I mean, if God had wanted him loose in the world he would *not* have blocked out our broadcast and millions would have seen the miracle. And then we wouldn't even be faced with this question. True?"

"YES!" the congregation roared as one.

"Hey," the preacher chuckled, "we can hardly kill somethin' that doesn't exist, right?"

That received wild hoots of "AMEN!" and "PRAISE THE LORD!" Several people rose from their seats and shouted with cupped hands, "Let's send him back to hell!" which received a hearty round of applause.

"Shew!" the preacher grinned, wiping his brow. "People, listen to me," he began with a new urgency. "A moment ago the Lord spoke to my heart." He paused dramatically, "Out of fire he came, and by fire shall he be dispatched *saith the Lord!*"

At that little old ladies and elderly men, brawny truck drivers, farmers, shopkeepers, laborers of every stripe, their wives and squeaky-clean teenagers became red-faced grotesque caricatures of themselves as they began to chant in one rhythmic roar, "Kill Satan! Kill Satan!" The preacher was almost dancing about the stage as he swayed to the rhythmic chanting, drunk with power and the lust for blood.

After a moment he held up his hands until the chanting faded, then began conversationally, "You know, used to the fires of hell as he is, dispatchin' him by way of fire is probably pretty humane." He paused, shouting, "And that is why the Lord will bless us with a third miracle tonight!"

The crowd cheered wildly.

"After the fire goes out," he screamed hoarsely, "the bones, skull, everything remainin' will simply vanish in no less a fantastic manner than that in which it appeared! And does everyone want to witness the third miracle?" he continued shouting as the crowd once again began chanting to the thunderous beat of their rhythmic stomping.

"Kill Satan! Kill Satan! Kill Satan!"

The Reverend Pat Patterson settled back on his heels with a big smile, allowing the audience to carry on for some time, all goose bumps as he exulted in the power of their collective chanting. Then he held his hands up and kept them up until the auditorium was deathly still.

"Now, my brothers and sisters," he said with quiet hoarseness, "there is one final thing we must determine. Please, everyone remain absolutely still and quiet in your seats when I ask this next question, because if there is only one dissenter among us I want to hear *him.*"

He paused until every sniffle and cough was stilled, then asked softly, "Is there even one single person who does not wish to witness the third miracle?" Sharp-eyed, brows furrowed, he scanned the audience of 5,000. "Please," he added, "don't be afraid. If you're out there and you do not wish to witness the third miracle stand and share your feelings with us."

Not one person rose.

The reverend smiled his delight but squelched the applause that started to build, waving them down with, "Hold it, now." He looked up at the little strip of mirrored glass, calling, "Tommy G., are you still with me?"

There was a click and buzz as the PA came on. "We can hear you loud and clear in here, reverend," the disembodied voice boomed out over the auditorium.

"Good, Tommy, thank you. Now, could you take a consensus of your crew for me and find out where they stand on this?"

"I already did that, sir, and the entire crew is with you 100 percent. And Ricky Brown wishes you good luck!" he added as a cheery afterthought.

"Thank you, Tommy G." The preacher turned back to the audience. "Well!" he laughed easily, "I'm glad we got that settled!"

All this time Cambian remained motionless, eyes downcast, standing with one foot on the other, shivering, arms drawn tightly to his sides for warmth. Now he looked up at the preacher.

Patterson caught the movement out of the corner of his eye and turned to the boy. "You look mighty chilly, son," he smirked. "Not used to air conditioning where y'all's from, eh?"

"No sir, I'm not," Cambian answered.

The reverend chuckled heartily, saying, "Well don't you worry none, 'cause we're gonna warm you up here right quick!"

"You're going to burn me at the stake?" Cambian asked incredulously.

"Well, I was thinkin' 'bout in the pig roaster," the preacher chuckled, "so's everyone can see the miracle."

Cambian almost laughed with the irony of his next thought. Back during the Vietnam war he had been deathly afraid of getting shot, but then when a renegade soldier had bludgeoned him to death with the butt of his rifle, well he could distinctly remember his surprise at how painless an experience it had actually been. After the first blow, of course. Perhaps it would be the same getting roasted alive.

Pacing easily about the stage, the reverend heaved a sigh. "Okay, I guess we're all in this together. Remember, not a soul is to ever know about this. It's a secret that, together, we'll take to the grave."

He gazed out at the congregation, his beady little blue eyes searching, but everyone looked somber and attentive. "Good. Now, are any of the maintenance men here tonight? Could you please stand up so we can see you?"

Three middle aged men stood up near the front center. As coworkers and friends they usually sat together. "Now I know you boys are all dressed up in your Sunday finery," the preacher began amicably, "but I wonder if I could persuade you to do me a favor and get our big ol' pig roaster out back and bring it up on stage with a goodly amount of wood?"

The three men nodded. "Certainly, reverend, we'll get right to it," one replied.

"Thank you, gentlemen. And don't forget," he cautioned as the men made their way to the aisle and started for the front side door, "not a word about this to anyone." And then loudly to the congregation at large, "We are all sworn to the utmost secrecy, people, and take heed not to forget at risk of eternal damnation." He paused, "Because if we handle *this* miracle well, there's sure to be more comin' our way."

As the maintenance men filed out to get the pig roaster the preacher changed tack, his voice growing louder, face redder as he pointed an accusing finger and shouted, "We know what *he* did to Jesus!" Snatching off his belt, he continued, "Why, I oughta warm his bottom a little before we roast it!"

The congregation roared with laughter and applause. They had Cambian down to Satan incarnate now, trying to jump in ahead of God's plan and thus hasten the approach of Armageddon. They themselves were to play the right arm of God. Become the executioners. In their warped minds it was biblical law, which they fancied themselves expert at—in the name of Jesus—which meant they could do no wrong.

After a brief debate they decided to strip him before the whipping for "scientific" reasons. To check out Satan's body before dispatching him back to hell. After all, it wouldn't be any more immoral than examining an insect, and when would they get the chance to see Satan again?

"Here, turn him this way," the preacher instructed the guards so the congregation could start out with a profile view. Gripping the back of Cambian's shorts, fist pressed firmly against the boy's buttocks, he snatched the shorts off with one sharp yank.

"Oh!" a man in the front row quietly exclaimed to another, "he looks just like any normal boy!"

"Oh yes," the other said, wagging his head, "but don't forget, he only *looks* normal, and looks can be deceiving."

The preacher turned with a big grin, holding the tattered shorts high like a trophy. And it was then that his business agent, Harry Wigglesworth, and Brenda May, his wife, suddenly got to their feet, walked hurriedly to the center steps and mounted the stage.

This stopped the preacher in mid-stride. With a confused looked he lowered the shorts, saying awkwardly, "Uh, just one moment."

For anyone to approach and mount the stage during a sermon was strictly verboten. And had it been anyone else but the man's wife and his business agent, a trio of security personnel would have beat them to the steps.

As they determinedly crossed the stage, he frowned at them darkly, stepped behind the podium, dropped the shorts and carefully replaced the mic in its holder. Turning and walking back towards the curtains at the rear, the belt still curled around his left hand, he waited with stern impatience.

Brenda May and Harry Wigglesworth joined him there, huddling so closely no one could see their faces. "Are you two crazy?" Patterson whispered harshly. "If it's gonna happen I gotta keep this thing hot and let the momentum carry us through!"

"But Pat," Brenda May began anxiously, "what's the percentage in it? I mean, we're not gonna make any money off'a burnin' this young'n!"

"What're you suggestin'?" he screeched indignantly, "that we turn Satan loose in the streets of America because we won't make any money off'a dispatchin' his ass back to hell?"

"No, Pat, it's not just that!" Wigglesworth excitedly broke in. "I mean, my God! Do you think you can really kill Satan with an ax or a bullet or a blowtorch? For God's sake, man!"

Patterson looked at him gravely. "Well I know that, Harry, and I have no illusions about killing it. Sure, it'll just come around again someday," and here he got loud, not caring if anyone did overhear, "BUT NOT ON THE LORD'S DAY!"

Harry Wigglesworth seemed to tremble and shake something off. Maybe the reverend *is* a prophet of God, he thought. Staring at Patterson, he bowed his head briefly and humbly said, "Yes, reverend, whatever you say. I leave it in your capable hands as a servant of the Lord Jesus Christ!"

Patterson straightened to his full height, drew a deep breath of forgiveness, and laid a hand on the man's head. "I will forget your moment of doubt and insurrection," he said kindly. "Go in peace, my brother."

Wigglesworth couldn't help giving another little bow as he and Brenda May humbly withdrew and returned shame-faced to their seats.

"And now, my brothers and sisters," the preacher pro-claimed, returning to the podium and discreetly slipping the belt on a shelf in back as he reached for the mic, "it's time to light the fire!" For some odd reason the whipping had lost its appeal. Now he just wanted to get this over with and see the miracle that he, in his utterly deluded, almost psychotic state, really believed would happen.

He patted his pockets, laughing self-consciously as he admitted, "I, uh, don't seem to have a match."

A moment later everyone was looking at one another, leaning over in their seats, whispers rising as everyone asked everyone else if anyone had a match. Nobody did. Nobody smoked.

"Oh shucks!" the preacher fumed, stomping a foot in frustration. To the congregation he asked with wide-eyed disbelief, "Nobody's got a match?"

Finally a young man of 18, starched white shirt, neat military haircut, stood and said, "Someone left a book of matches in my car, reverend."

The preacher looked at him and laughed. Wagging his head, he leaned forward and inquired with a pleasant grin, "Then what're you waitin' for? Go get them!"

The boy immediately jumped up. "Yes sir," he said rev-erently, then hurried off up the aisle as fast as he could without running. It wasn't polite to run in church.

He returned shortly with the matches, enjoying the warm glow of the limelight as he gained the stage. Taking a moment, he turned back to gaze out over the multitude from the great height of the mountain whose summit he had finally claimed, if only briefly. As one of the priests judging the 12 tribes of Israel he would probably have his own army to command with a private estate at least as big as the Christian Condensed campus, he mused. And his own private jet, just like the reverend. His head swirling with dreams of glory and power to come, he started across the stage to deliver the matches.

At stage center, starter fluid in hand, the reverend was liberally dousing the wood that had been carefully arranged in the pig roaster, the guards standing to one side with the naked, shivering child between them.

The irony of it was that at this point Cambian was *glad* they had decided to kill him. Not that he was too thrilled about being roasted alive, but after all, how bad could it be? He might die of shock within seconds of being put on the grill. Even so, if worst came to worst it would only be a matter of minutes and then he'd be back home playing in the pool with the girls. And these weird sickos could have his body and eat it too, for all he cared. Cambian chuckled with the thought.

The preacher looked up sharply, gave a last spray of starter fluid, handed the empty can to his match-bearer and turned to Cambian. "You'll be laughin' out the other side of your face here in just a minute, boy!" he snickered darkly.

Technically Cambian should have cautioned the man against carrying out his plans. Not for his own benefit, but for the preacher's and his very ill congregation. But the thought of pleading to this man for his life was too repulsive for him to even consider. Plus, he suspected in review it would be determined that it wouldn't have done any good anyway, so instead he opened his mouth big and laughed in the reverend's face.

"That's it!" the preacher cried as he spun and snatched the matches from the clean, starched Christian boy. "Ladies and gentlemen!" he bellowed hoarsely, holding the matches aloft, "from the fire he came unto us, and by the will of God and fire shall he depart!"

A wild cheer went up, the crowd hooting and hollering as the Reverend Pat Patterson turned to the pig roaster and with a great flourish, struck a match and tossed it in. There was a *whoosh!* as the fluid-soaked wood burst into flames, a puff of heavy black smoke roiling to the ceiling as the fire began to crackle merrily.

"And now!" the preacher cried, his face gleaming with sweat and wild-eyed excitement, "witness the third miracle!" Grinning triumphantly, he turned to the guards. "Gentlemen," he said, holding his hands out palms up and raising them.

One guard stooped and took Cambian by the ankles, the other under the arms, then they lifted him up, carried him to the pig roaster, and held him suspended above the blackened rack sizzling with grease, the fire crackling fiercely now, dancing flames only a few feet from the boy's back.

Bug-eyed and frightened, his naked body gleaming with sweat that dripped hissing into the fire, Cambian gritted his teeth. In a few minutes he'd be back home. He could hardly wait.

The crowd was chanting to the thunderous beat of their stomping feet, "KILL! KILL! KILL!"

The preacher hesitated, giving the crowd one of his most endearing grins, then looked at the guards and slowly lowered his hands.

But before the grill-iron seared Cambian's flesh all four sets of triple doors at the back of the auditorium slammed open as police and media stormed in, guns drawn, flashbulbs popping, TV camera lights glaring.

As troopers armed with shotguns quickly sealed off all exits the senior officer ran down the center aisle for the stage, gun drawn and shouting angrily, "Put that boy down, *now!*" He bounded up the stage steps as the guards quickly complied, swinging Cambian clear of the pig roaster and setting him on his feet. "And get those handcuffs off him!"

The reverend was looking inexplicably delighted as the chanting of the crowd quickly changed to frightened exclamations of surprise, all experiencing a sudden dread sense as if they'd just got caught playing with themselves.

Steadfastly maintaining his composure, the reverend grinned, calling reassuringly, "Now, now, brothers and sisters, have no fear. This is all in God's plan. Let's not forget who we are...."

As two patrolmen joined their superior on the stage and ordered the security personnel to lie face-down on the floor with their hands behind their heads, the senior officer snatched the mic out of the reverend's hand, spun him around and ordered, "Take off that jacket!"

"Officer, you're makin' a big mistake," the reverend intoned. "I'm the prophet spoken of in Revelations and this here," he gestured at Cambian, "is Satan."

"Yeah, and I'm Alice In Wonderland," the officer quipped, then roughly yanked the jacket off the man's back and kicked his feet out from under him, the reverend landing on the carpet with a loud thud. The officer immediately turned and squatted before Cambian. "Here, put this on," he said, helping the boy slip into it and securing the three buttons. "Would you like me to call an ambulance, son?"

Cambian, warm now in the big man's suit coat which hung down below his knees, smiled and shook his head. "No thanks, sir. I'm all right."

The officer chuckled delightedly. "Well you're certainly a tough little guy," he said, truly amazed. "You don't even seem shook up!"

"Things could have been worse," the boy shrugged.

Shaking his head in disbelief, the officer stood up and wagged a finger at him, "Now you wait right here and we'll get you out just as soon as possible, okay?"

Cambian nodded and smiled, "Thank you, sir."

The officer turned around and spoke loudly into the mic, "Would Ricky Brown come down to the stage, please?"

The reverend sat slumped on the floor, shoulders sagging, gazing at Cambian dully. Somehow this was all Ledyard's fault. His own son had done this to him. Why? That gave him an idea. He jumped to his feet and approached the officer in command. "Sir, I've got a sick boy in the hospital I've got to attend to."

The officer turned and stared at him.

"I've got a sick boy," the reverend repeated impatiently and started to walk off.

Grabbing him by his tie, the officer drew him around in a tight circle back to where he'd been, said, "Sit," and kicked the feet out from under him again.

"You don't know who you're dealin' with," the reverend threatened from the floor. "I did a miracle tonight!"

"Yeah? Well do one now and shut up!" the veteran police captain said, then turned to greet a young black man approaching from backstage.

"Hi. I'm Ricky Brown."

The officer stuck his hand out, "I want to thank you for making that call, Rick, you did the right thing."

Ricky rolled his eyes and grinned, "Well, under the circumstances the right thing wasn't all that hard to figure out."

"Well that may be, Rick," the officer said reflectively, "but there must be over 5,000 people here. Only one called." He jerked a thumb at Cambian, who, exhausted, had sat down cross-legged on the carpeted stage. "That's the boy whose life you saved. Why don't you go talk to him for a minute and we'll get you both out of here as quickly as possible."

"Thanks," Ricky said.

"Oh, by the way, did you call the media, too?"

Ricky Brown nodded, "The newspapers, radio, and TV."

"Why?" the officer asked out of curiosity, adding, "they almost beat us to the door!"

Ricky grinned and winked. "A story this big? They'll probably reward me with a job at the TV station when this is all over."

Chuckling, the officer shook his head again and turned back to the prayerful, weeping congregation and spoke loudly into the mic, "Quiet everyone, quiet please. I have an announcement to make." When it had grown reasonably quiet he continued, "You are all under arrest for conspiracy to commit murder."

A huge groan rippled through the crowd, as if they'd just been told they would have to stay after school.

CLOUD DROPS

23

CLOSE ENCOUNTER OF THE REAL KIND

> *Many will say to me in that day, Lord, Lord,*
> *have we not prophesied in thy name? And in*
> *thy name have cast out devils? And in thy*
> *name done many wonderful works?*
>
> *And then will I profess unto them, I never*
> *knew you; depart from me, ye that work*
> *iniquity.*
>   *- MATTHEW 7:22 - :23*

Doctor Beasely turned to his assistant in astonishment as they watched the evening news. "It, it can't be!" he stammered.

Pavlavi, his eyes big and round behind his thick glasses, continued staring at the screen. "I think they are in very bad trouble."

"Hah!" Beasely's laugh was a contemptuous bark. "That's the understatement of the year! First thing tomorrow you get that Patterson boy out to the state hospital, because I can tell you one thing for sure, we aren't going to be seeing any of *our* two grand a week out of this thing."

Pavlavi glanced at him and nodded. "First thing."

"Just tell them he's a paranoid schizophrenic controlled by whatever we're giving him."

"Aggressive/violent?" Pavlavi looked at his boss.

Beasely was taken aback. "Well was he?"

Pavlavi pondered a moment, then caught his superior's eye and shrugged, "I don't know."

"Then don't put it in."

*   *   *

Nationwide, Monday's papers had front pages splashed with graphic photos of the naked, handcuffed Oriental boy held suspended above the flames of the pig roaster by two hulking security guards in Christian Condensed uniforms, blond crewcuts, automatic pistols strapped to their waists. And this wasn't supermarket tabloids, but respected publications like the *New York Times* and the *Chicago Tribune*. The networks had a field day with their own graphic footage. And there was one long interview that had run repeatedly when the story first broke, of Ricky Brown describing Ledyard's prediction of the miracle.

The world was stunned. Protesters in Japan gathered in the streets, once again demanding the closure of American military bases. The Russian Ambassador to the United States got on the tube and in a simule-cast to the motherland, stated that he saw no violence in America's streets and that everyone was really quite friendly. The House of Commons cried for further restrictions on American television imports to England.

Within the week a lot of the televangelists, even some of the biggies, were off the air as donations trickled to zero. Even the few still airing programs looked pretty sickly, while people in the streets made bets over which would be the next to fold.

The Reverend Pat Patterson was held without bail. Brenda May and Harry Wigglesworth couldn't raise the five million each they needed, and so all languished in the same county prison awaiting arraignment on a variety of charges that included attempted murder and child sexual abuse.

For his part Granger fared somewhat better than the rest. Having departed that very Sunday evening on one of his jaunts to Switzerland, he had missed the event entirely and only learned of it from a CNN report after landing in Europe. Now, with access to more than ten million dollars in a secret Swiss bank account, he decided there was no point in returning to the States and was presently lounging on a nude beach in the Mediterranean with an 18-year-old in one hand and a cocktail in the other.

*   *   *

Under close questioning in a secured room at County Hospital, Cambian's response that he was 48 years old and had just dropped in from heaven made the assemblage of doctors, lawyers, and detectives chuckle, but that's when they phoned the state mental institution and told them to get a private room ready for a very special guest.

By all appearances he was just a very disturbed adolescent boy. Polite, nonviolent, drug-free. An apparent psychotic without the usual sidebars of depression or emotional disturbance. This in itself made his an extremely unusual case and they simply wanted to observe him. There would be no treatment program. In the meantime detectives would try to uncover his identity. He was a healthy, good-looking kid. Surely somewhere brokenhearted parents were frantically searching for him, although pictures on television produced not a single claim. But the detectives weren't worried. There had to be paper on this kid *somewhere*. Nobody just *poofs!* into existence.

*   *   *

The moment the darkly handsome Oriental boy entered the room Ledyard, although heavily sedated, knew he was looking at the one who had come for him in the wheel of fire.

Ledyard was in the common room when they admitted Cambian to the hospital. The doctors, of course, had no idea the two boys had previously met, nor, obviously, the fantastic nature of the encounter. Ledyard hadn't told them anything about his lifelong experiences, let alone his meeting with a Being in a wheel of fire.

Under the circumstances the doctors and investigators were extremely curious and had arranged the "chance" meeting in the common room to see what would happen. Although the little Oriental boy had previously claimed to know Ledyard as a friend, when Ledyard saw Cambian's image on television he flatly denied ever having met or seen him before. And the truth was, Ledyard *hadn't* recognized him, as he had never before seen him in the flesh, the television, of course, being unable to convey the multitude of unique qualities that would render Cambian recognizable in person. Furthermore, Ledyard hadn't seen the miracle, only heard accounts of it from church members interviewed on TV insisting they had witnessed the arrival of Satan cast down to Earth.

"Some miracle," Ledyard had muttered at the screen, adding sarcastically, "good goin', Lord, that miracle did everyone a lot of good!" With all that had happened he didn't know what to believe anymore. He was just one sad, very confused boy.

But when Cambian walked into the room and caught his eye, a huge, knowing grin on his face, Ledyard knew instantly—it was *him!* And then he bolted across the room and threw his arms around Cambian in a tight embrace.

Dumbfounded, the doctors and detectives observing scribbled furiously in their notebooks.

After Ledyard released Cambian and stepped back, he gestured at the bank of vending machines with a trace of longing and commented, "I'd buy you a coke, but I don't have any money."

Cambian shrugged. "I guess things aren't that hot in the miracle business these days, eh?"

And then both boys burst out laughing.

From the author of *Cloud Drops,*
Harmony's Angel, and **STRANGE CHANGE,**
— Other Dreams —
The second novel by
Nicholas Ifkovits

Randy "Taterhead" Ellis is a simple soul who raises chickens and sells the eggs in a small, rural Illinois town. When three adolescents, attempting to cover up a minor misdeed of their own, have him arrested on false charges of sexual impropriety, the community is outraged. Released by the courts, his business destroyed, property vandalized, the young man attempts to rebuild his shattered life, but the incensed community, feeling the legal system was too lenient in its resolution of the case, begins plotting its revenge....

A spine-tingling suspense drama, *Other Dreams* is about an American community gone mad with the dark, sadistic ravings of the witch-hunter. It's about the victims. It could be about you. Remember, sometimes dreams really do come true. Watch out which ones come true for you.

ABOUT THE AUTHOR

A graduate of Northern Illinois University with a B.A. in media communications, Nicholas Ifkovits is a member of the Golden Key National Honor Society in recognition of scholastic achievement, and recipient of the Outstanding Scholar Award presented by the Department of Communication Studies, NIU.

For his volunteer work with incarcerated youth he received a Certificate of Recognition from the Illinois Youth Center, Illinois Department of Corrections, and has seen his share of the darker side of the human psyche, including close encounters with serial killers Larry Eyler and John Wayne Gacy.

Other Dreams isbn 0-9651700-3-9 at bookstores now.
See first chapter at: **www.abookshops.com**

Harmony is abandoned by her mother. She never knew her father. After three years of living hell on Chicago's west side with an abusive uncle and his wicked family, the now tough, plain-spoken 16-year-old has decided it's time to get out—before it's too late.

This is the story of a runaway girl who <u>doesn't</u> end up a prostitute on drugs walking the streets of New York or LA. She ends up in love. With a boy. Together they flee Chicago in a boxcar on a westbound train with a black kid. A fugitive of the law. Now they're all on the run, to an encounter with....

Harmony's Angel has it all. Romance. Adventure. And the physical and spiritual struggle between good and evil that every man, woman, and child of conscience is engaged in.

About The Author

Nicholas Ifkovits has published a variety of novels that appeal to everyone, young and old alike of every stripe from ages 9 to 99. Part of the allure is the genre-diversity of his novels, which range from suspense to fantasy to adventure and romance. The author garnered attention for **Strange Change**, *Other Dreams,* **Cloud Drops** and *Harmony's Angel* through relentless touring for bookstore signings. Word-of-mouth from surprised and delighted readers did the rest. (-:

Strange Change, the 4th novel by Nicholas Ifkovits....

What are *your* fantasies? And what if you could act upon them? STRANGE CHANGE will return you to that twilight time between childhood and adulthood in a fantasy about a young man who discovers he has the incredible power to become anything he can imagine himself to be. And what he wants to be is in the girls' locker room at school at shower time.

And that's just for starters. He quickly learns that, with a thought, he can get whatever he wants, and compel others to do his bidding to an astonishing degree. As a result, his parents are practically his servants, his friends as subjects to royalty. But do his powers come from heaven, or from hell? As long as he gets what he wants, does it really matter?

About The Author

Nicholas Ifkovits was born in Chicago where he was raised until the age of nine, when the family moved into the shadow of O'Hare Airport in the Western Suburbs. A university graduate with a B.A. in media communications, he worked briefly as a videographer for a network affiliate in Rock Island, Illinois, before achieving success as a writer with his first four novels, **Cloud Drops,** *Other Dreams,* Harmony's Angel, and STRANGE CHANGE. His various novels and screenplays don't fall neatly into one genre, but cover a broad spectrum, from suspense to fantasy to romance and adventure. Get them all and see.

Strange Change isbn 0-9651700-1-2 at bookstores now.
See first chapter at: **www.abookshops.com**